MOTHER NUMBER ZERO

MOTHER NUMBER ZERO

MARJOLIJN HOF

Translated by
Johanna H. Prins and Johanna W. Prins

Groundwood Books • House of Anansi Press

Toronto   Berkeley

First published as *Moeder nummer nul* by Marjolijn Hof
Copyright © 2008 by Marjolijn Hof
Amsterdam, Em. Querido's Uitgeverij B.V.
English translation copyright © 2011 by Johanna H. Prins and Johanna W. Prins

Published in Canada and the USA in 2011 by Groundwood Books

Groundwood Books / House of Anansi Press
110 Spadina Avenue, Suite 801, Toronto, Ontario M5V 2K4
or c/o Publishers Group West
1700 Fourth Street, Berkeley, CA 94710

Publication of this book has been made possible with financial support from the Dutch Foundation for Literature.

We acknowledge for their financial support of our publishing program the Government of Canada through the Canada Book Fund (CBF).

Library and Archives Canada Cataloguing in Publication
Hof, Marjolijn
Mother number zero / Marjolijn Hof.
Translation of: Moeder nummer nul.
ISBN 978-1-55498-078-9 (bound).--ISBN 978-1-55498-079-6 (pbk.)
I. Title.
PZ7.H68Mo 2011   j839.31'37   C2010-905899-2

Groundwood Books is committed to protecting our natural environment. As part of our efforts, this book is printed on paper that contains 100% post-consumer recycled fibers, is acid-free and is processed chlorine-free.

Cover illustration by phil / i2iart.com
Design by Michael Solomon
Printed and bound in Canada

For Janny

• 1 •

Each one of us isn't so unusual looking, but anyone who sees us together knows immediately that we don't all match. My mother is blonde and has blue eyes. My father has gray eyes, stubbly red hair and a bald spot on the back of his head. My sister is Chinese. She has dark eyes and straight black hair. And then there's me. My hair is brown and wispy. My mother says I have honey eyes. That's stretching it a bit. My eyes are brown, but not really brown. It's as if they ran out of eye color when I was made.

At our house nobody looks like anybody else. That's not a problem. It's always been like that, so I'm used to it. But our names *are* a problem.

Mine is awkward — Fejzo. Nobody knows how to pronounce it and so they call me Fay. That's no help, because Fay is a girl's name.

My sister's name is a disaster. She's called An Bing Wa. Even Chinese people think it's weird. An Bing Wa means something like Peace-Loving Ice Baby. My sister was found in January, in China, outside in the freezing cold. She was taken to an orphanage and the people there called her Ice Baby. Here, everyone calls her An, but I always say Bing, and when I want to make her mad I call her Ice Baby.

"You should have given us new names," Bing once said to my parents.

"We didn't want to do that," my mother said.

"Why not?" asked Bing.

"Because those names belong to you," my father said.

"Because you only had your names and not much else," said my mother.

"But we did have *some* things," I said.

"As you know," my mother answered, "you had clothes. And An had her own little blanket. And you had a squeaky toy, Fay."

"Tell me again what happened to my little blanket," Bing said.

My mother shook her head slowly.

"It was a drama," my father said.

"It was a very dirty little blanket," my mother said. "I put it in the wash and it fell apart."

"Did I cry?" asked Bing.

"No," my father said. "I don't think you missed it."

"But I cried," said my mother. "I was so upset. It was your little blanket and I wrecked it."

"She bawled for a whole week," my father said. He imitated my mother's voice, "Oh, that blankie! That poor blankie!"

I didn't have to ask about my squeaky toy. It was still in one piece. It was lying in the drawer under my bed. If you looked carefully you could see that it was a little dog. It had been all squeezed and dented out of shape.

– – –

When I was in fifth grade we talked about where babies come from and their mothers. About what a grandmother is and a great-grandmother and a great-great-grandmother. I was given a chart with empty boxes. I had to place everyone somewhere in those boxes. It was fun, because I like to put things in order. I started with myself. After that I went to the box for my mother. I didn't know what to do next.

"I was adopted," I told my teacher.

"That's no problem," she said. "We'll just create an extra box."

My chart got two mother boxes. In the first box I wrote *mother 1*, for my first mother. In the other box I wrote *mother 2*, for my mother now. Right away I felt bad. My mother now had suddenly become number two. Quickly, before the teacher could read it, I erased it all and filled in the boxes again. In the first box I wrote *mother 0*. In the second box, *mother 1*.

"Do I really belong to you or not?" I asked my mother when I came back from school.

"You are my son," she answered. "Forever. The only difference is that you came out of someone else's belly."

I was happy that she was mother number one. When somebody asked me what it was like to be adopted, I explained it the way she did. I said I'd been in another belly.

Of course I sometimes wondered about mother number zero. But not very much. I belonged with my father and mother now, even though I was born somewhere else.

I think that from the very beginning Bing was always more curious. A Chinese parasol hung from the ceiling in her room, and she owned a pair of Chinese pajamas.

"Why don't you get a Chinese tattoo?" I said.

She pointed at her butt. "Here?"

"No!" said my mother.

"Yes, right there," I said. "Get a dragon."

"But it has to be a big one," Bing said. "A mini dragon would be useless. You'd barely see it."

"Big and colorful," I said. "So it catches your eye. Red, green and blue."

"And yellow," Bing said.

My mother looked relieved. "You're overdoing it. I don't believe you anymore."

"Overdoing it?" said Bing. "It's my butt and I can do what I want with it."

"It's also a little bit mine," my mother said. "I wiped it for years."

"All mothers do that," Bing said. "That doesn't mean a thing."

— — —

Bing is the oldest. Just before her first birthday my parents boarded an airplane. They were going to pick up Bing from China. At the orphanage they sang "Happy Birthday," and Bing began to scream like crazy. My mother has told this story at least a hundred times. Not all the stories she tells are true, but this one is. If you heard my mother sing, you'd understand why.

I came later. My parents didn't have to go on a trip. I was born in the Netherlands. But like Bing I came from another country. My mother number zero lived in Bosnia and I was in her belly. Mother number zero didn't want a baby. She couldn't take care of me and that was the reason she gave me up. Luckily she didn't give me away to somebody in her own country, because they had a war and far too many problems. She was smart enough to come to the Netherlands, and I traveled along in her belly.

Sometimes I thought about how it could have been. I imagined a country with houses ruined by war. Maybe I would have lived in one of those houses if my mother had stayed in Bosnia. But mostly those thoughts were buried somewhere deep down in my head. All children come out of a belly and nobody can remember that. What's the difference – one belly or another? One place or another?

• 2 •

We were going to the park. Hamid had borrowed his brother's leather soccer ball and wanted to practice taking shots. Jesse tied the scarf of his favorite team around his head. On the way to the park entrance he tried to keep the ball up in the air, but he kept dropping it.

I carried my drawing supplies. I wanted to look at the birds.

The aviary is at the entrance to the park. It has all kinds of birds – parakeets and many more. I'm not so good at the names of the smaller birds. They're too nervous and flappy. I'm into the big birds. I know them all. There are chickens, turkeys and guinea fowl, and even a couple of peacocks. They walk around on the loose.

"You were going to be the goalie," Jesse said.

A fat gray turkey sat still in the grass, waiting.

"Later," I said.

"Really?" Jesse said.

"Forget him," said Hamid.

He tugged at Jesse and they walked away together. The bridge to the playing field was at the other end of the park. I knew they weren't mad. They're used to it. I've known them since first grade and they understand me.

— — —

A girl was sitting in my usual spot. It would have been better to sit somewhere else, but I didn't think of that until it was too late. I'd already plunked down on the bench next to her, and I didn't dare get up again right away.

"What are you doing?" she asked.

I pretended not to hear her. I pulled a pencil out of my pocket.

"You're going to draw," she said.

I couldn't pretend not to hear her the whole time, so I said, "You guessed it."

I love to draw birds because they're complicated. At first they look kind of messy. Take chickens, for example. They just roam around. You don't know what they're going to do next and you don't really care, because the life of a chicken isn't all that exciting. But if you look really closely you notice how beautiful they are. The feathers are layered on top of each other in a special way. It's a lot of work to draw them, but I like the challenge. There's a system to it, but each time you have to rediscover it. When you start drawing, everything about a chicken makes sense. I like to draw other animals too, but they don't walk around by themselves. Usually they belong to people.

Jesse once tried to get me to draw cars. I'm useless at cars. For some reason a car never turns out right. Cars are what they are. Just like that. There's no point in taking a second look.

— — —

"Cool," said the girl.
"Yeah."

"I mean it." She pointed at my drawing and then at the turkey that was now walking around a little distance away. "That's the one. I can tell."

I went on drawing without saying anything.

"I like turkeys best," she said. "Their heads are ugly, but the rest is beautiful. The feathers are so special. They're like…" She hesitated a moment. "Little wreaths. Sort of wreaths on top of each other."

I glanced over at her. She had blonde hair. It was really short.

"Is that weird?" she said.

I didn't know what she meant.

"That I think turkeys look nice."

"No," I said. I'd never met a girl who thought turkeys were nice, but I didn't think it was weird.

"What's your name?" she asked.

I hesitated between Fejzo and Fay. I chose Fay.

"Nice name," she said. "I'm Maud."

"Nice name," I repeated.

"I have to go home," she said. "To help with the boxes."

"What boxes?"

"The boxes with all the stuff. We just got here."

She turned her face to me. "It was fun that you came over to sit with me."

"I always sit here."

"What's the name of this park?" she asked.

"Agathe Park."

"Who is Agathe?"

I shrugged.

"And Fred Walton?" she continued. "Who is he?"

"No idea," I said.

"I live on Fred Walton Lane," she said. "That's why."

— — —

At home I wanted to go on the Internet, but Bing was in the computer room in the attic and she wasn't planning to leave. She said she was doing her homework.

"Not true," I said. She was typing a note that didn't look very much like homework.

"I just started," Bing said.

"Not true, not true."

I was bluffing, but there was a good chance she was telling the truth. I'd been in the park all afternoon. After Maud went home, I'd played goalie for a while with Hamid and Jesse, and all that time Bing had the computer to herself.

She gave me hardly any room to sit down. She stood right behind the chair looking over my shoulder so I'd know that I had to hurry up.

"If I get a bad grade, it's your fault," she said.

I quickly typed *Fred Walton* on the screen. Bing often got bad grades and I didn't want to be blamed for it.

There were three Fred Waltons. The first was an American movie director, the second a wheelchair supplier and the third the inventor of linoleum. I knew immediately that number three was the one for Fred Walton Lane. Not far down the road, on the other side of the tracks, there was a linoleum factory.

– – –

It was a good thing I'd looked this up, because the next day Maud was sitting on my bench again.

"You want to know who Fred Walton was?" I asked.

"Well," she said, "who was he?"

"The inventor of linoleum."

"I didn't know you needed an inventor for that."

I sat down beside her. I put my sketchbook between us. "Everything needs an inventor."

She nodded. "But linoleum is so blah."

For a while it was quiet. It was my turn to say something, but I couldn't think of anything. For the first time I really looked at Maud's face. I noticed freckles, and little blonde hairs in her eyebrows. I noticed her ears. She was wearing tiny hoops. I quickly glanced at her eyes. They were blue and they looked back at me.

"Can I see your drawings?" she asked.

I pushed the sketchbook a little in her direction.

She took it and turned the pages one by one. "Birds and birds and birds. Is it for school?"

"No," I said. "For myself."

"This one's awesome." She put her hand on the drawing of the turkey. She had slender fingers. I kept looking because I wanted to avoid looking at her eyes again. All of a sudden she seemed too much of a girl. I stood up.

"What are you going to do?" she asked.

"Not much." I ran down the path, over the bridge to the playing field.

— — —

Hamid and Jesse were sitting on top of the goalpost. Jesse was tapping against the metal with a stone.

"Who is that chick?" they asked.

"What chick?"

"That chick you were talking to."

"Just somebody," I said. "I don't know."

"Does she have tits?" Jesse asked.

"Breasts," I said.

Hamid jumped down from the goal. "If you want to know whether a girl has tits," he said to Jesse, "go and look for yourself."

"Breasts," I said.

"Not necessary," Jesse said. "She's coming this way."

I turned around. Jesse was right – Maud was coming. She had already crossed over the bridge. She was carrying my sketchbook under her arm. I raced to the path. I was a bit out of breath when I arrived.

Maud held out the sketchbook. "You forgot this."

"Thanks," I said, without reaching for it. Now that she was standing in front of me, I saw that she was quite a bit taller than I was. She had no breasts. Almost. I didn't want to look, but I did anyway. Two small mounds under her T-shirt, that was all.

"And who do we have here?" said Jesse.

Bing was wobbling toward us over the bridge. She insisted on wearing high-heeled shoes, whether she could walk in them or not.

"Come home!" she called.

"What for?" I called back.

"You have to!"

"Why?"

"You have to go to your wart appointment!" Bing called. "That's why!"

I turned around, looking as surprised as I could. Was she talking to me? Of course not! I had no idea what this was all about.

"The wart - ap - point - ment!" Bing shouted. "Are you deaf or something?"

"Who is that?" Maud asked.

"My sister," I said. My voice sounded funny. I grabbed the sketchbook out of her hands.

On my way over the bridge I gave Bing a push. "Thanks a lot, Ice Baby."

• 3 •

It was Bing's turn to do the dishes and I wasn't
going to help her.

"I'm leaving," I said to my father.

"Back at eight o'clock?"

"Nine o'clock."

"Quarter past eight," my father said.

"That's toddler time."

"But you are a toddler!" Bing shouted from
the kitchen.

We had cauliflower for dinner and the pan
was badly crusted with cheese sauce. It couldn't
go into the dishwasher. Bing wouldn't be done
anytime soon.

– – –

I took Oak Street to the park. I knew nobody else would be there. Nobody I knew, that is. Hamid had swimming almost every night. He was on the water polo team and was a super fanatic. And you never saw Jesse outside after dinner. I had no idea what he was up to at that time.

On the long path to the bridge a woman was walking her dog. I took a right turn to the aviary.

First I looked to see whether the homeless man was there. He was usually hanging around on a bench. Sometimes he would stand near the duck pond. Jesse called him a bread thief, a dirty bread thief. I could care less. The ducks were fat enough. The bread thief could grab as much bread as he wanted, as long as he stayed away from me.

Jesse said he had a knife. And that he didn't only steal bread from the ducks, he stole the ducks too. No turkeys, because that would be too obvious. He killed the ducks with the knife, and at night the rats would gnaw on the bones and feathers.

I was always afraid that some day the bread thief would get tired of just stealing bread and ducks. And if I happened to be around then, he might get it into his head to kill a boy. I knew it was crazy. But still, when I went to the park by myself, I always checked first to see if he was there. Just to be sure.

All the benches were empty. I went to sit in my usual spot. I had left my drawing supplies at home, but that didn't matter. Just looking was good enough. A peacock dragged its tail over the ground. The gray turkey walked back and forth.

Just as I was kind of drifting off, I heard something behind me. Before I could turn around a hand grasped my neck. The bread thief! For a second I was sure it was him. He wanted to strangle me. I held my breath, panicking. The hand was warm and the fingers were slender. Then I heard giggling.

"Scared you, didn't I!" Maud said.

"I wasn't scared," I said. "Why should I be?"

"You're lying," she said.

"Nyeah," I said. I was good at that, saying yes and no at the same time. It drove my mother crazy.

Maud sat down next to me. "Where do you have warts?"

I moved over.

"Can you show me?"

"No," I said.

She fumbled with her shoelace. She took off her shoe and her sock. She stuck out her bare foot. It was long and skinny with a dirty sole. She had a large wart on her heel.

"This is mine," she said. "I have to go to the doctor, but I don't want to. I'm afraid it will hurt. Does it hurt?"

"Not too much. Just a bit."

"Your sister is Chinese," she said. "Or Japanese or something."

I couldn't keep up with her. First it was warts and now Bing.

"I saw it right away," Maud said.

"She's Chinese."

"Is she illegitimate?"

"Of course not." Sometimes I wished Bing didn't exist. But I didn't want anyone to say anything mean about her.

"An illegitimate child," Maud said. "That's what you call it, isn't it? That's when your mother isn't her real mother. Or is your mother Chinese too?"

"My mother isn't Chinese," I said. "My sister was adopted."

"That's what I thought," Maud said. "Wow." She put her foot up on the bench. "Wow," she said again. "And what about you?"

I didn't answer right away. I wasn't sure what I wanted to tell or not tell.

"You too?" she asked.

"Yes," I said. "We're both adopted. My sister and I."

She was quiet for a moment. She moved her toes up and down.

The gray turkey walked past the bench. If I reached out my hand I could pet it. But I knew it wouldn't like that even though I'd never tried. Everybody knows turkeys don't like to be petted.

"But where do you come from?" asked Maud.

"The Netherlands."

"The Netherlands?"

"I was born in the Netherlands, but I came from somewhere else."

"I don't get it," she said.

It was none of her business. I looked at her

wiggling toes and at her ankle and then for a second at her face.

"Because there was a war," I said. When I saw that she still didn't get it, I added, "Because everything was destroyed. Because my mother couldn't stay there."

"Oh," she said. "Sorry."

"What do you mean?"

"Sorry about the war and that everything was destroyed."

Sorry was all wrong. Sorry had nothing to do with me and nothing to do with mother number zero either.

She was still staring at me.

I couldn't stare back that long. I looked at her nose, her forehead, her ear, her lips. I tried to avoid her eyes. And then all of a sudden, I'd had enough. Enough of the way she said sorry and the way she kept staring at me.

I pointed at my watch. It was just past seven thirty.

"I have to go home," I said.

"Already?" asked Maud.

I wanted to walk away and leave her sitting in

the park, but I thought of the bread thief. Maybe he was hungry for a girl. The rats would eat Maud's bones. And her wart too. The bread thief would leave her wart behind. Nobody would dare put a wart in his mouth.

"Are you going to stay here?" I asked.

"Maybe."

"You can walk with me," I said.

She put her sock and her shoe back on. She wasn't in a hurry.

"Up to the traffic light," I said.

— — —

We walked out of the park together. A short stretch along Oak Street to the street crossing. Maud dragged her feet a bit.

"What's it like being adopted?"

I told the story about the other belly.

The pedestrian light was green. I wanted to cross but Maud stayed on the sidewalk, and because she was talking to me, I stopped too.

"Don't you want to know?" she asked.

"What?"

"Don't you want to know whose other belly it is?"

"Not really."

The light switched to red.

"I'd want to know," Maud said. "I couldn't stand not knowing."

A single car passed and then the intersection was empty. I jaywalked to the other side, toward the supermarket.

"Wait a minute," Maud called.

I waited until she caught up with me.

"Where do you live?"

I waved my hand. "Somewhere over there."

"Right there?" she said, as if she could look straight through the supermarket.

"Sort of," I said.

For a few seconds she was silent and I thought that I could go on.

"I like you," she said suddenly.

I had no idea what to say. I had no idea what to do.

"Well, bye," Maud said.

"Bye," I said.

She went one way and I went the other.

•4•

It was way too early to go to sleep. I took my animal book out of the closet and lay down on my bed with my clothes on.

The animal book was secret. Kind of secret. My father and mother knew about it and Bing too. But no one else.

– – –

It all began with *The Hare* by Dürer, a postcard of a painting my father once sent when he went to Vienna. A hare painted a long time ago, because Dürer lived from fourteen hundred something to fifteen hundred something. He had painted that hare very carefully. You could see he wanted to do it exactly right. All those tiny hairs were different – long and fuzzy on the hare's stomach, and short and a bit ruffled on its head.

Later on I discovered there were lots of painters of animals. Sometimes my father and mother would go to a museum, and once in a while I'd go along. Everywhere we went we bought postcards. I pasted them into a book and that became the animal book. *The Hare* by Dürer was my favorite postcard. There was another one I liked a lot, a small bird that looked almost real –*The Goldfinch* by Fabritius.

Maybe the animal book was like the squeaky toy, or the little blanket. Sometimes I slept with it under my pillow. Even my father and mother and Bing didn't know about that.

I loved the postcards and the way I'd pasted them into the book. Always two on a page, one below the other. Next to each card I wrote the name of the painter, always with the same pen, so all the names were the same color.

– – –

I looked through the animal book thinking about Maud. I didn't want to think about her. I'd rather banish her from my head. Or even better, from the park. Why couldn't she hang out somewhere else? She said she liked me. She said it herself. At our school nobody did that. A girl would send a friend over to you and you wouldn't have to do anything. You'd just say yes or no and that was it. Hamid had said yes and now he was going with someone, but you never saw them doing things together. They almost never talked to each other.

Maud did it differently. She didn't go to our school, but that didn't matter because she didn't have to send anyone over to me. She just said smack in the middle of the street that she liked me, without blinking an eye. I didn't answer, but what would I do if she started saying it again next time?

Once we had a thrush's nest in our garden. It had baby birds in it. They were always peeping, with their beaks wide open, and the parents had to stuff food into them all day long. Maud was just like one of those peeping baby thrushes. She would say this and she would say that and the whole time I had to keep flying over to give her something.

Halfway through the animal book I had pasted in a black-and-white postcard. It showed goats and people sleeping, and in the middle, a cow taking a piss. *The Pissing Cow* by Nicolaes Berchem. I didn't really want postcards with people, but the cow was fantastic and you hardly noticed the people. It often made me laugh, but not this time.

I put the book under my pillow and tried to fall asleep. All those glued-in cards so close to my head usually calmed me down.

— — —

Someone must have turned off the light in my room, because in the middle of the night I woke up in the dark. I took off my clothes and crawled under the covers.

The next morning my mother said, "What happened? I went in to check on you at midnight and there you were, muttering with all your clothes on."

"I don't mutter," I said.

"Oh yes, you do," she said. "You were muttering and mumbling. You were terribly restless."

My mother was right. It had been a restless night. The animal book hadn't helped much.

"It was nothing," I said.

"Are you all right?" my mother asked.

"Nyeah," I said.

She grabbed my shoulder.

"No or yes?"

"Nyeah," I said.

She squeezed me in her arms and started to tickle me. "No or yes?"

"Nyeah! Nyeahnyeahnyeah!"

"Now get out of here!" she said.

— — —

After school I went to play soccer with Jesse and Hamid. We passed the aviary. Maud wasn't there. I didn't see her anywhere.

Just past the bridge was a bunch of girls lying on the grass. They had chips and cans of pop and they called out to Jesse, "Hey there, you big hunk!" And then they couldn't stop giggling.

Jesse kicked the ball up in the air and tapped it from one foot to the other. Twice, before he missed. He pretended he'd done it on purpose.

Hamid and Jesse started playing soccer. I was the goalie and let all the balls in. I dove to the left or to the right and it was always the wrong way. The girls didn't stay long. They wandered over to the bridge, leaving their empty cans in the grass. Hamid and Jesse kicked one of the cans back and forth. Hamid aimed at the goal and I dove in the wrong corner.

"You're not paying attention," said Hamid, and he was right.

I wasn't paying attention to the can. I kept looking at the bridge. I was sure that Maud would turn up, but she didn't come. When we went home the park was almost empty, except for the bread thief.

— — —

That night it was my turn to do the dishes. I was lucky — we had pizza for dinner. Four plates, cutlery and a salad bowl. That was all. I didn't even have to turn on the dishwasher because it wasn't full yet.

Bing got mad. "You should do them again tomorrow," she said.

"Tomorrow it's your turn," I said.

"Fay's right," my father said to Bing. "And I'm going to cook tomorrow. I was thinking about three kinds of vegetables and a sauce and fried fish and a dessert with lumpy custard and baked fruit."

Bing stormed up the stairs to her room. She banged the door shut.

"Was that really necessary?" my mother asked.

"She ought to be able to handle a joke," my father said.

— — —

I left as fast as I could. I took my sketchbook along to the park.

The bread thief was spying on the ducks, but there was no reason to be afraid. There were lots of other people around. They were bowling on the lawn near the bandstand.

Two guinea fowl walked along the path. They didn't interest me. Speckled animals are too difficult. Speckles always look as if you'd invented them yourself. Luckily after a while a peacock came over. I took my pencil and tried to copy everything – the head, the body and finally the tail.

Once in a while I looked toward the path. Maud hadn't shown up. I remembered what she'd said about turkeys. About the feathers – wreaths of feathers on top of each other. I wished she'd come. First I hoped she wouldn't, but then I hoped she would. I wanted to show her my drawing. Maybe she not only liked turkeys, but peacocks too.

– – –

I was already on my way out of the park when she walked up.

"I was just leaving," I said.

She pulled the sketchbook out of my hands. "Let me see."

The peacock drawing wasn't done yet. The tail was only half finished.

Maud traced the lines carefully with her fingers. "I've been thinking."

"Oh," I said.

"About your mother," she said. "Your real one. Maybe she's a famous artist."

"A woman artist."

"Maybe she's world-famous."

I stretched out my hands because I wanted my sketchbook, but Maud pulled it back.

"You should find out," she said. "You're so good at drawing. I don't know anyone as good as you are. That must come from your mother."

"How would you know?" I asked.

"Can your sister draw?"

I thought about the sheets of paper with Bing's messy scribbles.

"No."

"And what about your father and your mother?"

"No."

"That's what I mean," Maud said. "You got it from somebody. From her."

"Why?"

"What else could it be?"

We walked to the park exit. Maud held on to the sketchbook.

"Give it to me," I said, because I didn't want to look like somebody who couldn't carry his own stuff.

But Maud walked on to the pedestrian

crossing. Then she pushed the sketchbook into my hands.

"You know what?" she said.

The pedestrian light was red. It was so crowded I had to stop. I was afraid that Maud was going to say again that she liked me, but she said something else.

"You should have this investigated. It's possible. Do you ever watch *Disappeared*? It's on TV every week. They search for someone's father or mother and then you can see what happens."

My mother didn't want us to watch that kind of show. *Disappeared* wasn't good for us, she said. At the end all those fathers and mothers who had reappeared would hug their children and everyone would be in tears. When Bing was watching, she'd cry too and she couldn't stop for a long time afterwards. I didn't like shows with people crying, and I wasn't too fond of Bing crying either.

Maud guessed right away. Could she read my thoughts?

"But you can also start looking yourself," she said. "Just you, without TV and that kind of thing. Don't you think?"

"Nyeah," I said.

We crossed the street.

"See you tomorrow?" Maud asked.

"I don't know yet," I said. "I may be playing soccer."

I walked home past the supermarket. Halfway I looked back. Maud was still standing at the pedestrian crossing. She raised her hand and waved. I didn't wave back. I kept walking as if I didn't care, but I felt itchy. My body was full of tiny waving hands.

— — —

In my room I leafed through the animal book.

Bing came in without knocking. Not completely though — she just stuck her head around the door. But she should have knocked, because a head is what counts. Once that's inside, the rest doesn't matter.

"Are you back?" Bing asked.

"How did you guess?" I said.

"How was the smooching?"

"What?"

"I know you, Fay," she said. "You're in love.

Have you been kissing each other?"

I didn't have time to answer. She closed the door. I heard her singing in the hallway. A ditty she'd made up.

> "There is Fay
> Up in the tree.
> K - I – S – S
> I – N - G."

"Ice Baby!" I shouted.

"Boy! You're missing that French kissing!" Bing sang.

"Not true!" I yelled.

"Stupid!" she shouted back.

I put the animal book under my pillow, but I knew it wouldn't help. My brain was in overdrive. *The Hare* by Dürer and *The Goldfinch* by Fabritius and even *The Pissing Cow* couldn't change that.

• 5 •

"Sleeping on it" is the stupidest expression I know. It doesn't help to sleep on something. Not for me. The next morning I woke up with a heavy head and a lot of questions.

There were the Maud questions. What should I do about her? Was I in love, as Bing said? I went to the mirror and looked at my face. It was pale, but otherwise it looked normal. Could you be in love without realizing it?

And what if Maud was in love? Most of all I was upset about the kissing song. Kissing was the last thing I wanted to do, even though Bing claimed I did. Kissing was really gross. Sticking your tongue into someone else's mouth and then tasting their spit. I shuddered to think of it.

Did boys start the kissing or did girls do it too sometimes? I couldn't ask Bing, because I was sure she'd die laughing. And I didn't want to ask Hamid and Jesse. It was none of their business and they wouldn't be able to help me anyway. They didn't know a thing about kissing. I'd never heard them talking about it.

And there were the mother questions. Was mother number zero famous? Did I like drawing because she liked it too?

The question about kissing would answer itself, even I knew that. I mean, everyone starts kissing at some point. But the mother questions would never be answered just like that. I didn't know where those answers would come from.

Or did I? A new question popped into my head. Did my parents know anything about mother number zero? Maybe they knew everything about her but had hidden it, because that's how it was done. Maybe that's how it was supposed to be when you were adopted.

– – –

On Saturday morning the four of us were having breakfast.

"Who was my mother?" I asked.

My father put down his knife. "Your biological mother?"

"Biological" was a dumb word. It made me think of organic rice and other stuff from the health food store on Main Street. Not a word for a particular kind of mother.

"Yes," I said. "That's the one I mean."

"We know very little," my father said. "And what we know, you know too. We've told you that."

I was relieved. They hadn't kept anything hidden from me.

"Is she famous?" I asked.

"What a question," my mother said. "What do you mean, famous?"

"Maybe she's a famous artist."

"Come on!" Bing said.

My father put his hand on her shoulder.

"I'm good at drawing," I said.

"And now you want to know whether she's good at it too?" my mother asked.

"Something like that."

"We don't know," my father said. "As I just said, we hardly know anything and even less about that."

"You'll never find out," Bing said.

My father's hand was still on her shoulder.

"It might be possible," he said. "If Fay wants to…"

My father and mother quickly looked at each other.

"Later," my mother said.

"Why later?" I asked.

"It's better."

"But it is possible?"

"It is possible," my mother said. "But…"

Bing interrupted her. She pushed my father's hand away. "Oh yeah? Is it possible? Great! Maybe Fay has a world-famous mother because he's so mighty good at drawing. Terrific."

I thought my father would get mad, but he let Bing talk.

My mother sighed. "An," she said to Bing, "Annie."

I didn't ask any more about mother number zero. I thought of Maud and I began to hate her.

Because she had started it all. I'd never want to kiss her. Never. I hated the thought of it.

— — —

On my way to the park I searched for words so they'd be ready if I needed them. I planned to stick up for myself. "Get lost!" That sounded good. "Why don't you get lost!"

When I found Maud, I lost my courage. She was sitting on my bench crying. I heard her sobbing. I wished I could walk away, but she'd already seen me.

"What's the matter?" I asked.

"I want to go home," she said.

"Why don't you go home then?"

"I mean really go home."

She snorted and when that didn't help she wiped the snot away with her arm. It wasn't hard to think that kissing was gross. Spit and snot. I'd rather swallow my own tongue.

"I want to go back to our old house. I don't know anybody here. Moving during middle school is the pits. They've all known each other forever and everybody is busy with the musical and the graduation party and nobody has time."

"At my school we're getting ready for a graduation party too," I said.

"Great." She said it a bit sharply.

"I understand," I said quickly. "It's a bummer."

"I really don't know anybody," she said.

"You know me."

"You're going to play soccer."

"Maybe I was going to play soccer."

Hamid had gone to a water polo match. Jesse had to be hanging out somewhere, but I hadn't seen him and I hoped he wouldn't see me. Not now.

Maud leaned toward me. "Can you tell I've been crying?"

Her eyes were swollen and there were red blotches on her face.

"Yes," I said.

She sobbed. "Then I'll stay here. I don't want to walk around like this."

I wanted to make her feel better. "I asked at home," I said. "About drawing and my mother."

She straightened up.

"But they don't know much about mother number zero."

I was startled. Mother number zero – those were my own words. I had written them down sometimes, but never said them out loud. And now I had.

"Mother number zero?" said Maud, as if it was the most normal name. "And?"

"I can look for her later."

"Later?" She looked a lot less weepy. "You can do it now too."

"I don't think so."

"It's not that difficult. You just have to start somewhere."

"In a museum," I said. I wasn't serious. How could you begin in a museum? Did the paintings come with name tags? *The Seagull* by mother number zero?

"Yes," said Maud. "In a museum."

I didn't say anything for a while. But it didn't matter, because Maud told a long story about a girl who was looking for her mother, and the only thing she knew was the country where her mother lived, and how she had traveled there and found her.

I thought about mother number zero. What if I found her? What if I just started somewhere and found her after a long time? What would I do? I'd go to her house and ring the doorbell and mother number zero would open the door. She'd recognize me immediately.

"Fejzo," she said.

Inside animal paintings were hanging on the walls. She had painted all of them.

"I'm so happy you came," she said. "I've been waiting for you for years and years."

She was beautiful. And she was soft and warm. Or not. Maybe she was ugly and smelly, because she painted all day long and never washed.

"Fejzo," she said. "I'll never let you go again."

She pressed me against her, and because she was so smelly I almost choked.

Or maybe it would be totally different. I would ring the bell and when she opened the door she wouldn't recognize me.

"I'm Fejzo," I said. "Your son."

She turned white and gasped for air. She dropped dead.

Maud had come to the end of her story. "So you see," she said, "if you just start somewhere, then you get more and more information."

"But we can't just start anywhere," I said.

"Why not?"

"Because."

"Do you have a better idea?" she asked.

• 6 •

My father was cooking and he'd made a royal mess. But it didn't matter, because I helped Bing with the dishes. I scraped off the leftover food and Bing loaded the dishwasher. After that we washed the pots and pans together.

"What's her name?" Bing asked.

"Maud," I said.

"Is she nice?"

"How would I know?"

Bing wanted to say something nasty. I could see it on her face, but she held back.

"And we didn't kiss," I said.

She waved the tea towel. "Of course not."

— — —

My father took Bing to her horseback-riding lesson.

"I'd like to have a little chat with you," my mother said. She had waited till we were alone. "Is something wrong?"

"No," I said.

"Are you sure?"

"Nyeah."

She put her arms around me. Not to tickle me, but to hug me. "You seem so different lately."

"Yes?" I said.

"Tell me what's wrong."

"My mother," I said. "Mother number zero."

She laughed softly. "Is that what you call her?"

"Yes," I said.

"Funny," she said.

"How can I find her?" I looked up at her face. "Is that bad?"

She tightened her arms around me a little more. "Of course not," she said. "I know that adopted children get curious sooner or later. That's very normal."

"Yes?"

"Yes," she said. "But perhaps you need a little more time to think it over."

"I've already thought about it."

"For how long?" my mother asked.

"Very long." I had only thought about it for a few days, and my mother wouldn't consider that a very long time. But I did, because I got sick of my own thoughts.

My mother let go of me so she could look me right in the eye.

"Listen, Fay," she said. "This isn't just a small thing. It might be much more complicated than you think."

"Why?"

"We know your mother lived through a war. We don't know everything. But when you begin to search…"

"So what?" I asked.

"There's a history with mother number zero and I'm sure it's not a pretty one. You're a bit too young for it. That's what I think."

I didn't know much about the war in Bosnia. People had been shot to death, but I didn't understand who the enemies were.

"We'll let it rest for a while," my mother said. "I also want to discuss it with your father."

— — —

Bing was gone so the computer was all mine. I was looking for pictures of animal paintings. I left the printer off, because only real postcards were allowed in the animal book. That was a rule I'd thought up. I found a painting bursting with birds — *The Floating Feather* by Melchior d'Hondecoeter. There were ducks and a pelican and lots of other things. As perfectly painted as could be.

My father and Bing came home. I heard them walking back and forth downstairs. Bing came upstairs and went into the bathroom. A little later my father came up to the attic. He sat down next to me. He smelled of horses.

"Well," he said.

I showed him the pelican.

"Beautiful," he said.

It took a while before he got going. I knew what he wanted to talk about.

"It's about your mother," he finally said.

I pushed the mouse over the deskpad and the cursor turned in circles on the screen.

"Are you very, very sure that you want to know about this? Have you really considered it long enough?"

"Yes," I said.

"Your mother doesn't think so."

"But I do," I said.

He stroked the bald spot on the back of his head.

"Hmmm," he said. "We expected this, but not yet. Sooner or later most children want to know where they come from. But honestly, we didn't know that it preoccupied you so much. It overwhelms us a bit."

"I can't help it," I said.

"We'll try to get some information," my father said. "But don't get your hopes up."

— — —

I walked down the attic stairs behind my father. I stopped at the door of Bing's room. I knocked. There was no answer. I knocked a little louder.

"Go away!" Bing said.

I opened the door and peeked inside.

Bing was lying on her bed. The Chinese parasol hung over her head.

"I said, go away."

"The computer's still on," I said. "It's your turn."

She walked over to the door and pushed it shut.

— — —

It was Saturday night so I was allowed to stay up late. I sat down on the couch between my father and mother. There was a movie on TV. It was a schmaltzy movie. My father and I tried not to laugh, but the more we tried, the more difficult it was. Every now and then my mother glared at us.

"Come on," she said.

A man with a moustache kissed a woman in an evening dress.

"Bring on the strings," my father said.

Slowly the music swelled. An orchestra of wailing violins.

"You see?" my father said. "There they are."

The woman leaned her head back and the man towered over her.

"Mmmm!" my father said.

"Ah!" I said.

Kissing on TV wasn't so bad. My mother looked offended, but I could tell she was faking it. "Thanks, guys. You're so macho. Bravo."

My father put his hand on her leg. "We're really mean."

But then we quieted down. We were sitting on the couch. My father, my mother and I. Mother number zero was there too. Invisible but nearby. I had talked about her and now she was with us. And she wouldn't go away again.

•7•

It was raining. My mother and Bing went to a flea market at the community center. My father wanted peace and quiet. He wasn't interested in the flea market or any other Sunday outing. I wanted peace and quiet too. I was stretched out on the rug in my pajamas with a shoebox full of stuff from the past.

Pictures of a young man with curly hair. That was my father. There was a picture of my mother in a short dress. She was trying to look beautiful with her mouth slightly open and heavy black eyelashes. Who was she trying to impress? I hoped it was my father.

There were later pictures too. My father in a car, and my father as a father, with Bing on his arm. She was leaning against his shoulder. A little blanket was wrapped around her. You could only see the back of her head.

I found a picture of myself as a baby, sitting on my mother's lap.

But there weren't just pictures in the box. There was also an envelope with birth announcements. Mine was light green. It wasn't a real birth announcement because I was born a while before the card was printed. It had a lot of information on it – when I was born and when I came to my father and mother and what my name was. And how incredibly happy they were to have me. That was in a little poem:

> He is welcome in our home
> And so welcome in our midst.
> We are truly deeply happy
> With him as our precious gift.

I knew my mother had written the poem herself. That's why I thought it was special. But one thing spoiled it. I pulled Bing's birth announcement out of the envelope and read her little poem:

She is welcome in our home
And so welcome in our midst.
We are truly deeply happy
With her as our precious gift.

I had once asked my mother why Bing and I had the same poem.

"Because we were equally happy with both of you," she said.

"Because your mother was proud she could produce even one poem," my father said.

Bing got hers first, so mine was secondhand. But my father said that made no difference. It didn't matter who came first. It was about the meaning of the words and they were equally true the first and the second time.

— — —

I put the birth announcements back in the envelope and returned the envelope to the box. I thought about the poem. I had read it before, but not in the same way. It said, "With him as our precious gift." It was very clear. The poem wasn't only about my father and mother, and how deeply happy they were. It was also about mother number zero. She had given me away.

My father was lying on the couch reading the newspaper.

"Dad," I said.

"Mmm?"

"Tell something about the first day."

He put the newspaper on his belly. "The first day of what?"

"The first day that I was here."

"Aha!" my father said.

I went over to sit on the floor next to the couch and leaned my head against his shoulder.

"You were almost four months old," he said. "And you had big eyes. And you looked around with those eyes. You looked and looked. I asked myself what went on in that little head. What did you see."

"I saw you and Mom."

"And Bing," my father said. "Bing was three when you arrived. She pinched your nose and you started to laugh."

"No," I said.

"Oh yes," my father said. "You started to laugh."

"Was I picked up by you?" I asked. "Or was I brought over?"

"Picked up."

Picked up. They had picked me up. That meant they'd seen mother number zero. Why hadn't they ever told me that?

"What did she look like?" I asked.

"Who?"

"My mother."

"I don't know," my father said. "We never met her."

"But how could she give me away if she wasn't there herself?"

"You weren't living with her," my father said. "You were staying in neutral territory. That's what it's called. A place that wasn't your birth mother's and not ours either."

Neutral territory sounded like something fenced in, a kind of storage place where mothers could leave their babies. That was horrible because all those babies needed new parents, and of course the cutest babies would be picked up first.

I tried to make a joke. "I guess you didn't have much choice?" I said. "I was the only one left."

My father wasn't fooled. He could tell I was kind of upset. He put his cheek against my head. "Cut it out, buddy."

He almost never called me buddy. It was an early pet name and I'd outgrown it.

"I'll tell you how it was," my father said. "Your mother couldn't take care of you, you know that. That's why she wanted to give you away. You need to understand that she didn't do it on a whim."

I pulled the paper from my father's lap and nestled close to him on the couch. I was too big for that as well, so we barely fit.

My father continued. "When you were born, your mother was given a few months' time to quietly think over her decision. She had to be absolutely sure that she didn't want to keep you. And while she was thinking, you had to stay at another home. We'd already been selected to adopt you, but it wasn't for sure yet."

"But I still think it's strange," I said. "She had

to think about me. Why wasn't I allowed to stay with her?"

"Because it would have been too difficult. She would have become too attached to you."

"But why couldn't I have gone to you then? I could have stayed with you until she had thought about it enough?"

"No," said my father. "If she had wanted to keep you after all, we would have had to give you back."

I thought of the little poem: "We are truly deeply happy."

"That's how it was," my father said. "We would never have wanted to give you back. It would have been a tragedy. That's why we had to have neutral territory. You had to stay with a family until the problem was solved, and that's where we picked you up when the time to think about the decision had passed."

— — —

Mother number zero had been given time to think it over. That I understood. I always needed a lot of time to think about everything. Small or big. She had been given time to think about something very important. But was the time to think it over gone forever?

I rang the doorbell and mother number zero opened the door.

"I've been waiting for you," she said. "I've been thinking very deeply and I want you back."

She pulled me inside. She pushed me through the hall and up the stairs. At the top of the stairs was a door, and behind it a room.

"Your room," mother number zero said. "Where are your things?"

"I don't want to stay," I said.

"I can't believe that."

"I want to go home."

"You *are* home," said mother number zero. "I knew you'd come. I knew you were longing for me just as much as I was longing for you."

"Time for thinking is over!" I shouted.

– – –

My father knew how to do it – how to spend a day doing nothing at all. He gave me a section of the newspaper. I went to the dining-room table and began the crossword puzzle on the last page. You shouldn't do crossword puzzles too often, but sometimes they can be fun. Because everything fits. If one letter is wrong, you've messed it up. I filled in the words with a pencil. Sometimes I asked my father, who was stretched out on the couch with the rest of the newspaper. He rustled the pages and sometimes read something out loud. It was just the right way to be together.

The puzzle was almost finished when I heard the front door slam.

"There are the girls," my father said.

My mother and Bing came into the living room. They had bought a lot of junk. My father acted as if he admired everything.

Bing had chosen a lamp for her night table, something with long ribbons and sparkles.

"So attractive!" my father exclaimed.

My mother had brought home a glass bowl and a vase and a couple of old coat hangers.

"So handy!" my father said.

"And here's something else," said my mother. She gave me a stack of postcards. "There was a man who had I don't know how many."

"It took us about an hour to find animals," Bing said.

I counted nine postcards. Four with fish and two with birds. There was one with a painting of two dead rabbits and one with a squirrel. The last card showed a white horse rearing up on its hind legs, with a man on its back. More a human card than an animal card. I gave it to Bing.

"Because you had to search for such a long time."

She imitated my father. "So outstanding!" she exclaimed. "Thanks so very, very much!"

— — —

Because it was Sunday, Bing and I didn't have to help with chores. After dinner I went up to my room. I was still walking around in my pajamas, and since the day was almost over I stayed that way. I got the animal book. It was a good thing I'd given Bing the horse rearing up. There were eight postcards left, and it worked out perfectly to paste in two on each page. It was too bad that most of the animals were dead. The rabbits looked limp. The fish would have looked better in a cookbook — one fish without a head had been cut up in slices. But the squirrel was alive and beautiful. Fluffy red fur, so natural that you wanted to touch it. I took my special pen and wrote down the name of the painter — Hans Hoffmann.

If I ever found my mother, I'd show her the animal book. She'd understand immediately.

I rang the doorbell and mother number zero said, "Please come in!" We sat down on the couch. I gave her the animal book and she opened it.

"*Red Squirrel*," she said. "Impressive. So lifelike and beautiful. And those fuzzy red hairs!"

"Beautiful, isn't it," I said.

"This one too," she said.

I moved a little closer so I could see it. "That's my favorite — *The Hare* by Dürer."

"That's my favorite one too," mother number zero said.

She pulled out a book and put it in my lap. It was her own animal book. *The Hare* by Dürer was in it and *Red Squirrel* by Hans Hoffmann and *The Goldfinch* by Fabritius.

"This one always makes me laugh." She pointed at *The Pissing Cow* by Nicolaes Berchem.

"I have that one in my book too!" I shouted.

We put our books next to each other. Two pages with *The Pissing Cow*. We both laughed.

"How did that happen?" I said when we stopped laughing.

Mother number zero stroked my cheek. "You're my child, aren't you?"

− − −

I closed the animal book and put it on my desk, far from my bed. As far as possible. I went downstairs. My father and mother were sitting on the couch watching TV. It was the middle of a soccer game. My mother leaned against my father. I sat next to her.

"Mom?" I said.

"What is it?"

"Nothing."

"Are you sure?"

"Mom," I said. "Mom, Mom, Mom, Mom, Mom, Mom."

"Come on," she said.

"Mom!"

She put her arms around me. "Just once more…"

"Mom."

She held me tight. She tickled my side. She knew exactly where to get me. I kicked my legs like crazy.

• 8 •

I hadn't seen Maud all day Sunday and I'd hardly thought about her. But on Monday morning I saw her when I rode my bike to school.

"Hi!" she called.

"Hi!" I called back and quickly biked on.

– – –

In class we talked about the graduation party. No musical but an evening of songs and dances and that kind of thing. Willem explained what he had in mind. He'd been our teacher for two years. He would miss us in the future, he said. He was hoping for a nice party with a lot of creativity and not too much karaoke, please, because that had become so old hat. He wanted to see original performances. We should prepare everything by ourselves, and he would stay out of it as much as possible.

"Karate," Hamid said.

"How?" Jesse asked.

"Like this," Hamid said. He circled his arms in front of his face.

"It needs something else," Jesse said. "Just karate isn't enough."

"A banner with Japanese letters," said Hamid. "A big one."

At home we had a sheet of paper with Bing's name on it. Peace-Loving Ice Baby in Chinese. I could copy the letters – Chinese or Japanese, it didn't matter much. Nobody could tell the difference and nobody needed to know where I got those letters.

"I can make something," I said.

"It's going to be a karate demonstration," Hamid said.

"Just the three of us," Jesse said. "Hamid, Fay and I."

"Sounds exciting," Willem said.

Hamid wanted to start practicing right that afternoon.

"I'm going to the library," I lied. "To look for Japanese letters. You need to practice, not me. I don't have to perform."

"Everyone has to perform," Jesse said.

"I'm holding up the banner," I said.

"Then you need to practice that!" Jesse said. "Because you have to hold it straight."

"There's nothing to hold up yet," I said. "And the party is still a long way off."

He shut up after that.

— — —

I went to the park with my sketchbook. There were women walking around with strollers and a group of girls sitting near the bandstand. Maud wasn't there. The bread thief was standing near the ducks. I acted as if I didn't see him. Turkeys and peacocks and a few chickens were stepping around on the grass. A rooster was napping in a little sand pit. I sat down on my bench, took my pencil out and got started. The rooster's beak was the most difficult. It was almost impossible to see how it fit together with that weird red comb falling over it. I had to erase everything a couple of times before I finally got it right. The paper got very thin.

The drawing was almost finished when I saw Maud coming along the path. She started talking even before she arrived.

"I knew it!" she called.

The rooster in the sand pit stood up, alarmed.

Maud sat on the back of the bench with her feet on the seat. "I knew it. Jesse said you'd gone to the library, but I knew you'd be here."

"I'm here all the time."

"Yes," she said. "But Jesse told me you had something to do."

Maud knew Jesse better than I thought.

"And he had no time either."

She'd just talked to him.

"You weren't here yesterday," she said.

"It was raining."

"It wasn't bad," Maud said. "We had an umbrella. It was so big it covered us completely."

She was still talking about Jesse.

"Oh yeah?" I said.

She began to whisper. She moved really close to me. "Jesse told me about the bread thief."

I didn't want to say "oh yeah" a second time, but I couldn't think of anything better.

"Sometime we'll take a look," Maud said. "Early in the morning when it's still dark."

It sounded like a Jesse idea.

"What are you going to look for?"

"Dead ducks," she said. "The bread thief is called a bread thief, but he really steals ducks and he kills them and then he eats them."

"I know that," I said. Maud didn't have to tell me what happened in the park. "He's dangerous."

"Really?" She sounded as if she liked the idea of something dangerous.

"The bread thief has a knife," I said.

"Of course he has a knife. How else would he kill ducks?"

I looked at the drawing of the rooster. The rooster itself had disappeared.

"I'm going to look for my mother," I said suddenly.

She sat up straight and shut up.

"I'm starting today."

"Now?"

I had no idea how and where I should start.

"Soon," I said.

Maud had forgotten about the bread thief. "Get your cell phone," she said. "I'll give you my number."

"I don't have a cell phone."

"You do too," Maud said.

I did have a cell phone, but I never carried it around with me. The battery had been dead for weeks.

Maud grabbed the pencil out of my hand. She wrote her number at the bottom of my drawing. "It's important. When we start searching, you should be able to phone me."

The rooster was ruined.

"Wow," said Maud. "I'm so curious about all this. About your mother and why she did it."

I wanted to say, the war. But then I remembered the talk with my father about time to think it over. Mother number zero had come to the Netherlands. She'd been given time to think about her decision, and it was here that she'd given me away.

"If I were you, *that's* what I would ask her," Maud said. "As soon as you find her."

Why had she done it? In wartime a baby can be a problem. I got that. You have to escape and hide from the enemy and a baby can cry at the worst times, even when the enemy is close by. But why had my mother fled and then given me away after all, when she was no longer close to the war zone? When she had had enough time to think it over quietly?

"And if I were your mother I'd tell you right away," Maud said.

"Oh yeah?"

"Right away. I'd tell how…"

"Who cares?" I tore the rooster drawing out of my sketchbook. And then I tore it to pieces. I put the shreds in my coat pocket.

"What are you doing?" Maud asked.

"Can't you see?"

I didn't give her a chance to say anything else. I walked out of the park without even looking back.

— — —

At the dinner table my father noticed that something was wrong.

"Tell me what's going on," he said.

"I want to look for my mother," I said.

"Yeah, we know all about that," Bing said.

"But now I'm serious."

"Can we have a quiet talk about it later?" my father asked.

"It's important," I said.

Bing pushed her plate away. "Can I be excused?"

"We're not finished yet," my mother said.

"But I am," Bing said. "And when I'm finished I get up from the table."

"An!" my father said. "Simmer down."

Bing stood up and left the room. The door slammed shut.

My father looked at his plate.

My mother shook her head.

"What's the matter?" I said. "What? Can I help it?"

"No," my father said. "You can't help it, but you have to understand what's going on."

He told me about Bing. How she was found

somewhere outside and how she was taken to the orphanage and then flown to the Netherlands. I'd heard all this before, but this time my father explained what it meant. Because Bing had been abandoned, she couldn't look for her mother. They'd made inquiries, but nobody knew who Bing's mother was. Nobody had seen her dropping Bing off.

— — —

I went upstairs and knocked on Bing's door.

"No!" she called out.

"I understand now," I said.

"Get lost!"

I heard her crying behind the door.

"Bing?" I said.

She didn't answer.

— — —

Downstairs my father and mother were doing the dishes, even though it was really my turn.

"Let's have a quiet talk," my father said.

"Just the three of us," my mother said.

They asked whether I was really sure about

wanting to look for mother number zero. And I said yes. They asked whether I was absolutely sure and I said yes.

"It's not that simple," my father said. "We don't know where your biological mother lives."

"Mother number zero," my mother said. "That's what Fay calls her. Mother number zero."

"All right then," my father said. "We don't know where mother number zero is. We don't know her."

"We don't know what kind of person she is and whether it's a good idea for you to see her," my mother said.

"That too," said my father. "There's a lot involved. We don't know whether anyone can find her."

"I just have to start somewhere," I said.

"Sweetheart," my mother said. "You weren't planning to look for her yourself?"

I didn't answer.

"I hope not, Fay."

"Suppose," my father said, "you find mother number zero. You'd never be able to, of course, but suppose you find her. Then what?"

"Then I'd meet her."

"No," my father said. "No, it doesn't just happen that way. You have no idea who she is. And she doesn't know you either."

"You need help with this," my mother said. "There's an office, an agency. There are people who can help with the search."

"We can make an appointment," my father said. "We can find out what they have to say about it."

"Let's do it," I said.

"You want to know for sure?" my father asked.

"Yes," I said. But I wasn't that sure at all. My head was split in two. One half was full of questions, and the other half didn't want to have anything to do with it. The half with questions won.

"Yes," I said, "for sure."

•9•

I charged my cell phone, and then I called Maud's number. I had put together the torn-up pieces of the rooster drawing.

"Yes?" she said.

"It's Fay."

"And?"

Silence.

"Fay?"

"It's about my mother," I said.

"Yes," Maud said. "Your mother."

"We're going to look for her," I said. "I just wanted to tell you."

"Are you going to start looking right now?"

"No," I said. "No. We can't. We have to go to a special office."

"Oh?"

"A search agency."

"Oh!"

Silence again.

"That's what I wanted to tell you."

"An agency?" Maud said. "So you're not going to find her yourself?"

"Yes, I am."

"No, you're not. You just said you're going to an agency. I don't get what you mean."

"That we're going to start looking."

"But who will do it?"

"The agency."

A long silence.

"Well," Maud said. "Good."

The conversation was over. Maud didn't feel like talking anymore. I could tell. She was mad because I'd left her behind in the park.

"Sorry," I said.

"Sorry about what?"

"Sorry about what happened."

"OK," Maud said. "Well, bye."

"Wait!" I said. "I have to show you something important."

"When?"

"Now."

"I don't know if I can go out now."

"Just for a second," I said.

— — —

I ran to my room to get the book of animals. Then I ran down the stairs to the front door.

"I'll be back in a sec!" I yelled, and before anyone could answer I raced down the street.

Maud was a hungry baby bird and I had a treat for her. I had a secret book. Maud was allowed to see it. She loved secrets, like words you didn't want to say and things you wanted to keep to yourself. She would love the book of animals.

We reached the pedestrian crossing at the same time.

"What's that?" Maud asked.

I thought we should sit down first. There was a bench across the street near the sidewalk. I didn't wait for the light to change. There was hardly any traffic. A man on a bicycle had to swerve to avoid us.

Maud plopped down on the bench. "What's that?" she said.

"It's a book."

"What kind of book?"

"It has painters in it," I said. "No, not painters. I mean paintings, of course." I stroked the cover of the book of animals. "Jesse doesn't know about it, and Hamid doesn't either. Almost nobody does."

"What kind of paintings?"

"Animals."

"Let me see," she said.

I opened the book, half on Maud's lap, the other half on mine. Maud looked. After a while I turned the page.

"This is *The Hare* by Dürer," I said. "From 1502."

I didn't know how long to wait before turning the page. Slowly I counted to ten. On the next page I pointed at the head of a deer. I read out loud what I'd written next to the card, "*The Buck* by Diego Rodríguez de Silva y Velázquez."

"It's a scrapbook!" Maud said.

I turned a couple of pages at the same time. "And here's a cow," I said. I didn't say it was a pissing cow. She could see that for herself if she looked carefully. But she wasn't looking at the book anymore. She was looking at me.

"It's a scrapbook!"

"It's a book of animals," I said. "It's a collection of animals. Well, of paintings of animals. Postcards of paintings."

"Why?"

"It's something special," I said. "Do you get it?"

"Is it your mother's?"

I stopped turning the pages. I stared at *The Pissing Cow*. "No."

"Whose is it then?" asked Maud.

"Mine."

"Nice," Maud said. "I used to have a scrapbook with dog pictures, but I lost it a long time ago." She got up. "I have to go home."

I watched her leave. I sat on the bench with the book of animals on my lap. Two boys on bikes crossed the intersection. I hoped they wouldn't see me. When they'd gone by I stood up. On the way home I walked past a trash can. I pressed the book of animals tightly against my chest.

•10•

Suddenly she was part of our group. All four of us were in the park — Maud, Jesse, Hamid and I. Jesse always knew what to say to Maud. He told her one story after another. He knew everything about everybody and Maud wanted to know everything about everybody, so they never stopped talking. Hamid said as much or as little as usual. He acted as if Maud had been around for years. She was allowed to play soccer with us because she couldn't win anyway. Her kicks were hard enough, but the ball went in the wrong direction. I stayed on the soccer field the whole time. I wanted to draw birds, but I didn't dare leave.

Maud and Jesse were making plans.

"Tonight we're going to see the bread thief," Maud said.

"What do you mean, we?" Hamid asked.

"Just us."

"We aren't going tonight," Jesse said. "We're going early tomorrow morning."

"That's almost tonight," Maud said.

"We have to wait till he's asleep," Jesse said.

"He needs to kill a couple of ducks first," said Maud.

"I'm not going," Hamid said.

"Why not?"

"Because it's stupid."

"What about you?" Maud asked me.

I looked at Jesse and Maud. I'd have to go with them.

— — —

I'd never snuck out of the house before, but it wasn't that difficult. I made almost no noise and nobody woke up. It was still pretty dark. The pedestrian light at the intersection jumped from red to green and back to red again without a single soul wanting to cross. I hoped there were no burglars hanging around the supermarket. Or murderers or even worse. My mother didn't want me to go out late at night, and I was sure I wasn't allowed out so early in the morning.

It took a while before Maud and Jesse arrived. They walked up together. I heard them chatting. Jesse was dressed all in black – pants, a sweater and a wool hat. There were black smudges on his face. Maud wore jeans and a long black vest.

"Why are you wearing that?" she asked.

I'd put on my jacket without thinking. Blue with lots of reflecting stripes. My mother thought it was important to be visible.

"Glow in the dark," Jesse said.

I took off my jacket, turned it inside out and put it on again. I couldn't keep my hands in my pockets because now they were on the inside.

– – –

On the way to the park Maud and Jesse kept chatting, but near the entrance they stopped.

"Whisper," Jesse said.

We snuck along the path, as close to the bushes as possible. Something stirred in the shrubs.

"Birds," I whispered to reassure everybody. "Or hedgehogs. Hedgehogs always make noise."

"Shut up now," Jesse whispered back.

Near the fence along the duck pond he signaled that we had to crouch. We squatted next to each other and peered through the wire mesh. We saw ducks, but they weren't dead. No bones to be seen.

"Those dirty rats," Jesse said. "They haven't left anything."

He pointed toward the playing field. Hunched over, we followed the path to the ditch. Slowly it got lighter. A thin mist hung over the water. We stopped at the railing of the bridge. On the other side, on one of the benches along the playing field, you could see a bulky shape.

"The bread thief," Maud said.

Jesse crossed the bridge first. Maud hesitated a moment. I pushed her aside because I was the last one, and I didn't want to be last. Not as long as we were near those rustling bushes.

– – –

We crept along the edge of the field to the bench.

The bread thief was asleep under his coat. He was snoring.

"He stinks," Maud whispered.

"He's full of booze," Jesse said in an even softer whisper.

There were two plastic shopping bags under the bench. Maybe there were dead ducks inside. Maybe a knife. No, not a knife. The bread thief's knife was under his coat, of course, ready to be pulled out.

Jesse leaned forward. The bread thief sighed.

Away! I waved.

But Jesse acted as if he didn't see me. His face was very close to the bread thief's.

Suddenly the bread thief opened his eyes wide and then his mouth too. "No!" he cried. "No, no!" He sat up straight and pulled his coat around him.

Jesse ran down the path and over the bridge.

"Fay! Come!" Maud said.

I wanted to go, but I couldn't. I had to stay and watch.

The bread thief began to moan, "Ooh." A trickle of drool came out of his mouth. He was toothless.

"Fay!" said Maud. She grabbed my hand and pulled me away.

"Dirty bastards," the bread thief mumbled. His voice sounded hoarse.

We ran across the bridge.

"Dirty rotten bastards!" the bread thief shouted after us.

— — —

Jesse was waiting just outside the park.

"I peed my pants," Maud said.

"He grabbed his knife," Jesse said.

"What on earth were you doing?" Maud asked me. "He just stood there," she explained to Jesse. "He was so scared, he just stood there!"

"The bread thief didn't have a knife," I said. "*He* was scared."

Jesse wiped his face with his sleeve. "He had a knife. I saw it with my own eyes."

"And he doesn't kill ducks," I said. "He doesn't have any teeth."

"What's that got to do with it?" Maud said.

"He can't chew without teeth," I said.

"But he really did have a knife," Jesse said.

•11•

"Where were you?" my mother asked. She was standing in the kitchen in her bathrobe.

"I was just outside."

She stepped right in front of me. "Why?"

"I was awake."

She looked stern. "Fay?"

"I couldn't sleep, that's all."

"Next time you'd better stay inside."

"Why?"

"I don't want you wandering around the streets," she said. "It will cause trouble."

My father came into the kitchen. "Trouble? After breakfast, please."

My mother shook her head. It meant my father shouldn't make jokes, and that meant something was wrong. Usually my mother shook her head when Bing was angry or sad, and even the smallest joke would set her off.

I didn't ask what my mother meant by trouble. Maybe she was afraid I was hanging around smoking and causing mischief. There was always a lot of vandalism at the playground around the corner.

— — —

It was still too early for school. I took a detour and biked through the park. Not many people there. A man throwing a stick and a large dog chasing it. A boy raking in one of the bird cages.

The bread thief wasn't lying on the bench anymore. I saw him standing on a small side path. He was peeing against a tree and he didn't look too upset. When I passed by on my bike he looked up.

"Morning," he said.

"Morning," I answered. Just like that. I'd never said a word to him before. I was glad that he was standing up and that nothing seemed to be the matter with him. Nothing extra, I mean.

Nothing that was our fault. He didn't look angry, or maybe he was angry, but not at me because he didn't recognize me.

— — —

I wasn't the only one with extra time. Jesse also got to school early. He was sitting on the little wall along the schoolyard. I didn't say anything about the bread thief's knife and Jesse kept quiet too. He started talking about the karate demonstration and about the banner I was supposed to make. I said the party was still a long way off. But Jesse said I had to hurry up. They had to practice. Real karate fighters practiced for years and years and the graduation party was only about eight weeks away. That was nothing. Time would fly. And that banner had to be ready as soon as possible to make it look more real when they were practicing. I'd agree with that, right?

"Sure," I said.

"Here," Jesse said. He shoved a plastic bag into my hands. It had a bed sheet inside.

— — —

There was no way around it. I needed Bing's name. After school I began to search. Somewhere in the dining room cupboard there had to be a sheet of paper with Peace-Loving Ice Baby in Chinese characters. There are Chinese people — calligraphers — who do beautiful writing. They make art with a word or a name. Once my mother took Bing to Amsterdam to see a calligrapher who lived over a Chinese shop. Every time my mother tells the story, she's the one who laughs the most.

Bing was very small at the time.

The calligrapher said, "Sweet girlie. An Bing Wa sweet girlie."

"Sometimes," my mother said, "An Bing Wa also naughty girlie!"

Bing has always claimed that she can remember all of it and that she felt totally embarrassed. I don't believe that for a second. Toddlers don't get embarrassed. Not until later.

I looked all over the cupboard. On the shelves, behind the doors and in the drawers. Nobody was home and nobody needed to know what I was doing. Certainly not Bing. In the third drawer I found a folder with Bing stuff. A few drawings and a stack of official forms. The sheet of paper with the Chinese characters was on top. I rolled it up carefully.

There was a folder for my stuff too. I would never have saved those things myself. Drawings of people with only a head and arms. One drawing had a dog with five legs. But if you looked very carefully, you could see that the fifth leg was really a tail.

In my room I copied the characters on a big piece of paper. It wasn't easy. Each one had several different lines. Some of the brush strokes were thick and others thin. Some brush strokes crossed each other. The first character looked like a small person, the second like the letter K with something strange in front of it, and the last character had two patterns that didn't look like anything at all. It took a long time before I got it right.

My mother and Bing came back home and I had to be careful. I heard Bing going up the attic stairs, and a little later my mother went to the bathroom. I snuck downstairs and put the sheet of paper back. Then I snuck upstairs again and right afterwards I came downstairs the normal way.

"I'm going out for a minute," I called.

"Wait a moment," my mother called back from behind the bathroom door.

I had my jacket on already.

I went to the park. Back to the park. I had my sketchbook, but it wasn't about the birds anymore. It was about Jessie and Maud. I needed to stay around them.

The bread thief was standing near the duck pond with his hands on the fence. He saw me coming. He raised his hand. Just a little. Not quite waving.

"Hi," I said. It felt almost normal to talk to the bread thief.

Just past the first bird cage I saw Maud and Jesse. They were kissing. I suddenly understood why Bing called it pecking. That's what it looked like. It didn't look like a scene from a smoochy movie — more like a strange kind of biting. I couldn't really see it. I didn't even want to look, but I knew that Jesse's tongue was in Maud's mouth and Maud's tongue in Jesse's. They were tasting each other's spit.

I walked back to the entrance of the park, past the bread thief.

"Hello, there," he said.

·12·

We were sitting around the dining-room table.

"This is kind of a family conference," my father said. He looked at me. "We're a bit worried about you. That is…we think you're worried."

"And of course that worries us," my mother said.

It already sounded complicated.

"Do we have to do this?" Bing asked.

"Is it about mother number zero?" my mother asked. "Or is it something else?"

I didn't understand why they wanted to talk about me with everyone there.

"There's nothing else," I said.

"We're planning to contact that agency," my father said.

"You're always roaming the streets," my mother said. "And sometimes you sneak through the house."

"That's another matter," my father said. "Let's not confuse the issues."

"I'm not confusing anything," my mother said. "I just have the feeling that something isn't right. I only wanted to say that Fay's acting a bit strange."

"I'm not acting strange," I said. "And you don't have to worry."

"You mean well," my mother said, "and it isn't that serious."

"Be that as it may," my father said to me. "If you're going to look for your mother, it has consequences for all of us. We all have to agree with that. An?"

"Yes," Bing said.

"I talked to An," my father said. "She understands."

"I can say that myself," Bing said.

"It's not a small matter," my mother said.

"Of course everything will stay the same," my father said. "But at the same time much will change."

"Dad!" Bing said.

"I mean our family will stay the same," my father said. "But if Fay is going to look for his mother…"

"You must be absolutely sure," my mother said to me. "And you can always stop."

It was an important moment. I understood that. I had to think it over and say what I thought. But all I could think of was Maud and Jesse and how they were kissing each other. I thought about the bread thief, who had spoken to me. Something was wrong with my brain. It was always thinking at the wrong time. Or about the wrong things.

Bing took a deep breath. "I find it difficult," she said.

"Of course, sweetheart," my mother said. "That's OK."

"It's OK with me too," I said.

Bing was trying hard not to cry. "I know you can't help it," she said.

"Maybe we can go and look for *your* mother," I said. "Maybe it's possible if you keep looking."

"But how?" Bing said. "It's forbidden to abandon children, especially in China. You get locked up in prison if you do something like that. So my mother would know better. She'll be careful not to get caught. She left right away."

"Wait a minute," my father said. "We weren't there and we don't know what happened."

"Lucky for you that you can look for your mother," Bing said. "Can I please be excused now?"

Nobody said anything. Bing walked out of the room. She didn't slam the door and she didn't stomp up the stairs. She went quietly to her room.

"I'll go see her in a minute," my father said.

"Are we done?" my mother asked.

"We'll see how things develop," my father said.

— — —

I lay down on my bed to think it over. Without the book of animals under my pillow. The book of animals didn't help anymore.

My mother had said that I should be certain, and that we could always stop. But that wasn't true. I couldn't stop. It was like starting on a difficult drawing. Nothing looked right. But I couldn't erase anything.

I didn't think about mother number zero the same way I did at first. I didn't imagine that I'd ring her doorbell and that she'd do this or that. I knew I wouldn't ring her doorbell because I wasn't going to search for her myself. Other people were involved now. My father and my mother and Bing. Maud. And Jesse, because I knew for sure that Maud had told Jesse everything. And soon the people at that agency would be involved too. The people who were going to help look. How would I be able to stop? I really didn't know if I wanted to stop, because I didn't know who mother number zero was. I wanted to know why she had given me away. I wanted to know more and more. It just went on and on. I could only stop if I knew everything, because I couldn't erase all those questions in my head.

I tried not to think about Maud and Jesse. Most of all I wanted to erase Maud and Jesse.

— — —

I went to Bing's room.

"Bing?" I said with my mouth against the door.

"Yes?" Bing said.

I opened the door carefully. Bing and my father were sitting on the bed. My father stood up when I went in.

"I'll leave the two of you alone," he said.

I sat down next to Bing, on my father's spot.

"I don't want to talk about it," Bing said.

"Me neither."

"Then what are you doing here?"

"Nothing," I said.

"Idiot."

Bing had black rings around her eyes. She had been crying and her make-up had run.

"You look like a panda," I said.

For a long time we said nothing. We sat next to each other on Bing's bed under the Chinese parasol. Bing knew what it was like to have a mother number zero. I didn't know anyone else who knew what that felt like.

My mother came upstairs with a bowl of popcorn.

"Is this a cozy get-together?" she asked.

Bing and I looked at each other.

"Oh yes," I said.

"Yeah," Bing said.

"That's nice," my mother said. "I'm happy about that."

Bing giggled.

"Are you making fun of me?" my mother asked.

"No," I said.

"Nooo," Bing said.

•13•

The strange thing was that Maud acted as if nothing was the matter. As if it was perfectly normal to say that she liked me and then to go and kiss Jesse. And now that she was into kissing, she couldn't stop.

We were almost never together on the playing field anymore, and so there were no more soccer games. When Jesse was in the park, Maud was too. They would sit together on a bench or behind the bandstand. Hamid and I stayed out of the way. I hung out at the entrance to the park and drew one bird after another. Sometimes Maud came by when Jesse wasn't around. Then she'd sit next to me and ask if I'd found my mother yet.

"Not yet," I'd answer.

"But when?" she once asked. "Will it take much longer?"

"No," I said.

That was all Maud wanted to know. I should have been glad that she was finally leaving me alone, but instead I wished that she would ask me a very unusual question. And that I would have an answer ready, without even thinking about it.

– – –

One afternoon the bread thief sat down next to me.

"Why don't you draw people?"

He smelled like booze and dirt.

"I only draw birds," I said.

"I'm a bird." He laughed. "A strange bird. And I want you to draw me."

"I can't do that."

"Aw, come on," the bread thief said. He walked over to the fence near the duck pond and turned his face toward me.

When you draw you have to look very carefully, so that's what I did. I really focused on the bread thief. On his head and his coat and the way he stood there, and I tried to put that down exactly right on my paper.

He got impatient. "Finished?" he called.

"Finished," I said.

It was a useless drawing. Nothing was right. Human beings aren't birds. The bread thief stood right in front of the bench and blew his smelly breath in my face.

"You can have it," I said.

"Well done," the bread thief said. "I never get anything. People look down on you a bit, you know, when you're a bum like me."

I wasn't in the mood to talk about what kind of a bum the bread thief was. I carefully tore the drawing out of my sketchbook and rolled it up.

"A bum!" the bread thief said. "I know that's what I am. You don't hear me bragging. Some people brag, but why do it, that's what I always say. If you've got nothing then you've got nothing, especially if it's your own fault." He carefully picked up the drawing. "You know," he said. "Lots of things can happen to you, but some people can handle it and others can't."

He stopped a little way down the path and

leaned over to get his plastic shopping bags from under a shrub. Then he disappeared in the direction of the bandstand.

— — —

Some people can handle it and others can't, he had said. That's how it was when you had to go through a lot. I was going through a lot lately, but not as much as the bread thief meant, for sure. And mother number zero? She had gone through a war and given her kid away. Maybe that was more like what the bread thief meant. Was my mother like some people who could handle it, or like others who couldn't? If she couldn't, then maybe she lived in a park somewhere too. Maybe she drank beer all day long and had a knife to kill ducks. Maybe that was the answer to the question of why she had given me away. She had gone through so much that she had turned into a bum. Maybe she was crazy. Or wounded or crippled. Maybe she didn't have a nose or only one leg or no arms.

The bread thief reminded me of something else too. If there was a mother number zero, there also had to be a father number zero. I wasn't stupid. I knew where babies came from. I had always known there must be a father number zero, but I had never really asked myself who he was. I came out of someone else's belly. That's the way we talked about it at home. But no one ever mentioned that I also came from someone's penis. And who knows there might be more. There could be brothers and sisters number zero. Brothers and sisters who were born after me or before me and weren't given away. And grandfather and grandmother number zero, they existed too. A whole world full of number zeros swirled around in my head. It was too much. One father and one mother were enough for me. And the grandfathers and the grandmothers that I knew, and Bing. One Bing was more than enough.

I could see it now – mother and father number zero and a bunch of kids. They lived in the park, all huddled together under one old coat. All of them had knives. There were hardly any ducks left.

Mother number zero moved over a little.

"Come and join us," she said.

"No," I said.

"You're probably looking down on me."

"No," I said.

"I know we're bums," mother number zero said.

"It doesn't matter."

"That's good. So then we can go home with you."

"I don't know if that would be OK with my mother."

She started to laugh. "Your mother? Are you in your right mind? Who here is your mother? Well?"

She blew her smelly breath in my face.

• 14 •

I started on the banner. I was allowed to work on it in the gym at school.

The sheet was pale yellow and had a flowery border on one side.

"We'll cut that off," I said.

"I wouldn't do that," Jesse said.

"Who has to paint the letters?" I said.

"Whose sheet is it?" Jesse said.

I wasn't in the mood to argue about it anymore. I started with the first character. First I painted the outline with black paint and a thin brush. I'd fill it in with a thick brush later. I knew that wasn't the right way to do it. Chinese people do it differently. They paint with big, flowing brush strokes, but I knew I'd never be able to pull that off.

Jesse was keeping the sheet stretched out. After a few minutes he'd had enough of it. He began dragging over all kind of things – a stool, a box of wooden balls and a rolled-up mat. He weighed down the corners of the sheet and then left me alone. That was fine with me.

It took me a long time to finish just one character and then I had to clean up the mess that Jesse had made.

– – –

I didn't go to the park. I biked straight home. My mother was sitting at the table. She'd made tea and put out a bag of cookies.

"I spoke with someone on the phone who will help you search," she said. "We can go see him."

"When?"

"The day after tomorrow."

The day after tomorrow was awfully soon.

"Will you come too?" I asked.

"Of course," she said. "Or would you rather…"

"No," I said. "No, you have to come too."

She took a bite of her cookie. It crunched in her mouth.

"Will my mother number zero be there?" I asked.

"No," she said. "First we have to talk. About how to set it up. About you. About everything. We can only talk for now. Is that all right?"

"Nyeah," I said. Because I understood that talking had to happen, whether I liked it or not.

My mother took another cookie, but she didn't put it in her mouth. She just held it in her hand.

"What's the matter?" I asked.

She put down her cookie. "It's like the beginning of a new chapter."

I understood what she meant.

"But it's not a problem," my mother said, "if we're ready for it. Are you ready?"

I had no idea what would happen, so how could I know if I was ready for it or not?

She took my hand. "We'll see," she said.

— — —

The weather was bad and so I stayed inside. The rain beat against the windows. It wasn't much better the next day. It went on and on. My mother was right. It was like the beginning of a new chapter. Sometimes when you watch a movie you can tell from the music that something's going to happen. You can see it too. The door opens just a crack, a strange light shines in, and outside the tree branches sweep back and forth. Then you know something's wrong, but the people in the movie don't have a clue. That's how I felt. I could see the signs that something was about to happen, but I didn't know what. The house, my room, myself. Nothing was the same. Even the weather had changed. I knew that was a coincidence, but it seemed like the rain was falling especially for me. I couldn't avoid it. Now it was going to get serious.

"Don't you want to go outside?" my father asked. "Get a bit of fresh air? It won't hurt you to get wet."

"Why don't you leave him alone," my mother said.

— — —

I sat in my room. Bing was in hers. My father and mother were downstairs watching TV.

If I found mother number zero, I would invite her over. She should know where I lived and how I was doing.

I took her upstairs.

"This is Bing's room," I said. "We aren't allowed inside. And this is my room."

I opened the door.

"Nice," mother number zero said. "But a little on the small side."

My mother brought tea and cookies and that was strange, because suddenly there were two mothers standing side by side, and I was there by myself.

•15•

We went on the train. It was crowded. A woman with a large bag on her lap sat across from me. There was a dog inside the bag. Another woman sat farther down. She wore a tight dress and I could see part of her breasts. Next to her sat a woman with sunglasses. I couldn't see what she was looking at. Maybe she was looking at me. She could be mother number zero, I thought. Why not? But the woman with the bag could be mother number zero too. Or the lady in the tight dress. I looked around. There were a lot of women in the train. In the back compartment, close to the door, there was one with long brown hair. I imagined her standing up and walking over to me.

"Fejzo? Is that you?"

I didn't answer right away. The people in the train were watching. They looked at each other.

"Fejzo? Yes! I can see it now. It's really you!"

I looked out the window. We were traveling past a field. There was no station nearby.

"I'm your mother!" the woman said. "What do you think of that?"

Halfway through she suddenly sat down. But now the woman in the tight dress stood up. She was wearing high heels and she stumbled in the aisle on her way over to me. Her breasts bobbed up and down.

"Do you see?" she said to the other passengers. "Look, I've found my son! Here he is!"

The woman with the bag didn't need to get up. She was sitting close by. She stretched out her arms and said in a hoarse voice, "Now I recognize you! You're not a baby anymore, but I recognize you. You're my Fejzo!"

I leaned back as far as possible.

This is how it would be when I met my real mother number zero. She'd be a stranger and I'd have no idea what to do. The train shook to the left and right. If it went off the tracks we'd never arrive, I thought. Then there wouldn't be a new chapter. Everything would stay the same.

— — —

The train didn't go off the tracks. It traveled on to the last station and everyone got out. My mother and I left the station and walked into the city. We walked close together, under an umbrella. We were both nervous. My mother passed all the shops without even looking in the windows. Usually she would try to sell me on a pair of pants or a shirt that I didn't like, but this time she wasn't interested in new clothes. She kept looking at the directions on the map she'd printed out at home.

We arrived too early, but it didn't matter. A woman let us in and showed us into the waiting room.

"Here we are then," my mother said.

"Are they going to ask me all kinds of questions?" I asked.

"I think so," my mother said. "But they have a lot of experience. They know what they're doing."

A young man stuck his head around the door.

"Fejzo?"

I stood up.

"Want to come with me?"

My mother and I followed him into a room. At the door he held out his hand. "My name is Jos."

I gave him a limp handshake, but I couldn't do it over because he'd already let go.

— — —

The conversation wasn't as bad as I'd expected. Jos asked questions. He wanted to know if I'd thought much about mother number zero, and I told him almost everything. Jos got it right away. He talked about other kids and what they often thought, which I also got right away. I had thought the same thing — that it could be great to find your mother or not so great. He also talked about the mothers. That sometimes a mother number zero didn't want to be found, or *couldn't* be found.

My mother listened too. We were in Jos's room for an hour and the whole time she sat next to me without saying very much. Sometimes she nodded. When Jos asked her a question, she answered. After the hour had gone by, we made an appointment for the next time.

"It would be good to talk to each of you separately," Jos said.

"I think so too," my mother said.

That was fine with me. I didn't care that much. I was glad the talk was over, and I didn't feel like thinking about the next time yet.

We were very quiet walking back to the station.

"Was it easier than you thought?" my mother asked.

"Yes," I said.

"I was surprised. You said so much."

It was the first time she'd heard all the things going around in my head.

"Is that bad?" I asked.

"Of course not."

"Do you mind that I'm thinking about another mother?"

"Of course not." She hesitated a little. "It's just a bit nerve-racking sometimes."

"It is?"

"I shouldn't have said that," she said. "That's not what it's about. It's about you."

I told her about the train. About the women. I hadn't mentioned them to Jos. I told my mother that not a single one seemed like a nice mother number zero.

"That woman with the shopping bag," I said. "She was really awful."

I left out the bobbing breasts of the woman in the tight dress. It seemed better not to mention that.

"The little dog in the shopping bag!" my mother said. She laughed.

On the train home we sat across from two women. One was wearing a hat and the other was reading a book.

My mother winked at me.

— — —

Dinner was ready. My father had done the cooking. At the table I didn't know if I should or shouldn't tell about the conversation, because Bing was there. My mother began.

"It went well," she said.

"That's great," my father said.

"It was quite far away," my mother said. She hesitated, keeping an eye on Bing the whole time.

"I'll hear more about it later," my father said.

Bing finished her plate without saying a word.

"Can I help with the dishes?" I asked.

"No, thanks," Bing said.

"Let me help you," I said.

"Don't overdo it."

"An," my mother said. "I understand…"

"We still have dessert," my father said.

I tried to make a joke. "Even more dishes!"

"We'll do them all together," my mother said. "Then it's no big deal."

"We'll do them all together," Bing aped her. "Then it's no-o-o big deal!"

"What's the matter with you?" my father asked.

Bing stood up. She pulled up her T-shirt and stuck out her bare belly. Her belly button was pierced.

"No," said my mother. "Please no. It's fake. An, say it's fake."

"It's real," Bing said.

"Why your belly button?" I asked.

"Why not?"

Bing pulled down her T-shirt.

"You shouldn't have done that," my mother said.

"Why do you care?" Bing said.

"I think you should go to your room now," my father said to Bing. "Right now."

"But what about the dishes?" my mother said.

"I was going to get a tattoo," Bing said. "But it's not allowed until you're sixteen." She looked at my mother. "A tattoo, that would have really ticked you off."

"An!" My father took a deep breath.

Bing was already at the door.

•16•

The second Chinese character looked easy, but because of that it was more difficult to paint. It was a big mess.

Jesse wasn't around. Hamid was helping with the sheet.

"It looks like a K," Hamid said.

"I still need to add something," I said. But I could already see it wouldn't work.

"Doesn't matter," Hamid said. "Nobody can read it."

Bing can read it, I thought. We'd all received an invitation with an RSVP. We had to say how many people were coming with us to the graduation party.

"The whole family's going," my mother had said.

Bing didn't protest. She had been punished and she was keeping quiet. My father had called the riding school to say that Bing wasn't allowed to take any horseback riding lessons for a month.

But one night I heard my father and mother talking in their bedroom.

"She needs support now most of all," my mother said.

I was on my way to the bathroom. I stood still and put my ear against the door.

"There are limits," my father said.

For a while they didn't say anything. My feet got cold.

"I don't know what's best," my mother said.

"Neither do I," my father said.

The next morning Bing was off the hook.

"I expect you to do your best," my father said.

"With what?" Bing asked.

"With everything."

Bing tried hard to do her best. When my father and mother were around she pulled down her T-shirt as far as possible.

— — —

"Are you going to paint another letter?" Hamid asked.

I shook my head. One was enough. "What do you think?" I asked. "Does it look OK?"

Hamid inspected the letters. "Well…" he said. "I think so."

"Are you sure?"

He lifted up the sheet's flowery border with his shoe. "Does this go with karate?"

"What do you think?"

"Maybe it won't show too much," Hamid said.

— — —

I went home to get my sketchbook. Then I went straight to the park. I didn't want anyone to bother me.

It was a special day for lawn bowling. People were playing near the bandstand and the bread thief stood there watching them. I walked quickly past him.

The birds were hungry. A bunch of chickens and roosters came running up to me. I chased them away. A goose was sleeping under a shrub, his head tucked under his wing. He lay perfectly still and I picked up my pencil. I'd only drawn a few lines when two hands covered my eyes. They were warm and they smelled of grass. I knew it was Maud.

"It's you," I said.

"Who is you?" Maud asked.

I pushed her hands away. She sat down next to me on the bench.

"What are you doing?"

"Can't you see?"

I drew the goose's body. Maud watched. Its neck was bent back and its beak was stuck under its feathers.

"A goose without a head," Maud said.

"It's asleep," I said.

"That's why," Maud said.

I hoped she'd go away, but she stayed right there.

"How's it going with your mother?" she asked.

"Good," I said.

"Has she been found yet?"

"No."

There wasn't a lot more to say. The conversation with Jos had seemed like such a big step, but nothing much had happened. I was waiting for the next time. That was all.

I kept drawing and after a while Maud got bored. She left me alone.

— — —

A few days later my father and mother went to see Jos together. I stayed home wondering the whole time what they were talking about.

"Jos is good," my mother said when she came back. "I trust him."

"I do too," my father said.

"But what did you talk about?" I asked.

"About you," my mother said. "About how we can help you best. And about us. About how we feel."

"How do you feel?"

"We're doing just fine," my father said.

"That's not an answer," my mother said. "Of course Fay's curious."

She put her hand on my shoulder. "We have to think about what will happen and what we need to do too. Jos is helping us."

"That's why it's meaningful to have a

conversation like that," my father said.

"Did you talk about Bing too?" I asked.

"Yes," my mother said with some hesitation. "About the best way we can help her."

I had gone looking for mother number zero and now everybody needed help. That's what it boiled down to. Everything got more complicated and bigger, and that didn't make sense somehow. That's not what I had wanted. I thought of Maud. How she made everything bigger and more important than necessary. And now I was doing the same thing. I wanted to say that they shouldn't visit Jos anymore. That they didn't have to be helped. Nobody needed to be helped because it was all a mistake. Mother number zero wasn't that important.

"Are you OK?" my father asked.

My mother hugged me.

"It'll be fine," my father said. "Just fine."

— — —

The next day it was time for my second conversation. My mother took me to Jos and then she went into town.

"Well," Jos said. "Everything all right?" He had a folder with loose sheets of paper on his lap.

"Yes," I said.

"Do you still have questions?" Jos asked. "About last time?"

"No, not really."

"No?"

"Will it be OK for Bing?"

"Who is Bing?"

"My sister."

Jos leafed through his papers. "An. I have here that her name is An."

"An is Bing," I said. The conversation was taking an unexpected turn.

"I can't say very much about An," Jos said. "But you don't have to worry about that. I'd rather talk about you today."

I didn't want to talk about me. How could I explain that to Jos? Maybe there wasn't enough of me. Not enough to make such a fuss about. It seemed like I was fooling everybody.

Jos asked questions and I answered them. We talked for a while about mother number zero. Jos explained how the search would be done.

We finished after an hour.

"We'll make another appointment," Jos said. "We'll keep on talking."

Still more talking.

"We'll do it soon." Jos stood up. "Monday afternoon?"

"I'll ask my mother if she can make it then," I said. It sounded so childish.

– – –

The time passed slowly. At school I painted the last character. It was difficult, because there were really two next to each other and both of them were complicated. The sheet had to dry for a day. After that I rolled it up.

I was feeling more and more upset about the next conversation.

"I'm going to take you there," my mother said. "And shall I go in with you then?"

"You don't have to," I said. "Why don't you do something else?"

"OK."

"But I don't want any more underwear," I said. She'd already bought me some the last time.

– – –

We went on the train for the third time. There were lots of women as usual, but I looked out the window. We got off and walked through the city. My mother took me to Jos. She stayed in the waiting room until he came to get me.

This time Jos didn't have many questions. He explained how things would go from here. Like everyone else he assumed we'd go on, and I kept my mouth shut. I was glad that I didn't have to say much.

Jos shook my hand. For the time being this would be our last conversation, he said. But I could call him anytime. In case something came up. In case I wanted to tell him anything.

"OK," I said.

•17•

"Now it's really begun, right?" my father said. "Are you excited?"

"Kind of," I said.

The search had begun, but it wasn't that exciting. It didn't feel like a beginning. To me it seemed more like a lot was finished. I didn't have to talk or make any more decisions. I didn't have to think anymore. It was too late for that now. For the first time in weeks I felt calm. My mother was worried.

"Are you anxious?" she asked.

"No," I said.

"I understand," she said. But she didn't understand. I should have been excited because mother number zero was almost found, but my head was empty. No, that's not true. Not totally empty, but more empty than before.

— — —

One night Bing came into my room.

"Can I come in?" she asked.

I wanted to say no because that's what Bing and I usually said when we wanted to get into each other's room.

"Yes?" Bing said. Her voice shook a bit.

"Yes," I said.

She sat down on my bed. "I'm going to China," she said.

"Not true," I said.

"Yes, it's true."

"But you can't go to China," I said. "You have to go to school and you don't have any money." I thought for a moment. "And you don't speak Chinese."

"That will come."

"So you're not going right away?"

"No."

"Too bad."

"But seriously," Bing said. "When I finish

school, I'm going."

"And then what?" I asked.

"I'm hiring a Chinese detective."

"They don't exist."

"You have Jos," Bing said.

"But that's different. Jos isn't a detective. Jos is…" I didn't know what Jos was. "Why don't you try on TV?" I asked. "On *Disappeared*?"

"Don't be stupid."

"They'll take you to China right away."

"Oh yeah?"

"Yeah."

"And then my mother will appear and then she'll tell how she left me outside. And then I'll tell how I almost froze to death. And then she'll tell how she ran away as fast as she could and that she could care less that I almost froze to death. And she'll say all this in front of a camera. For sure!"

I didn't know the part about Bing almost freezing to death. It was the first time I'd heard that.

"I'll use a Chinese Jos," Bing said. "I'll have him do the search."

"But there is no Chinese Jos!"

She looked at me. "You have to believe in it."

"But how…"

She stood up and walked out of the room.

"I believe it!" I called quickly.

"Not!" Bing said.

"Yes!" I called. "I do believe it." I followed her but she was already in her own room and the door was closed.

— — —

I was dozing a bit with my hands behind my head. My mother woke me up.

"Do you know where An is?" she asked.

It was late. Outside it was getting dark.

"She was here," I said. "But that was a while ago."

"How long ago?"

"About an hour?" I guessed.

"Did she say anything?"

"Something about China."

My mother walked through the house, opening and closing all the doors. I followed her around, but I was sure that Bing wouldn't be hiding in the bathroom or in the broom closet. She tried to call Bing on her cell phone. With an angry face she repeated the message, "…An…I'm not in right now…Bye."

"She's probably with a friend," my father said.

"I don't have their numbers," my mother said. She sent Bing a text message. Of course there was no reply.

My father wanted me to go to sleep and I went to my room. A little later I heard the front door slam. I looked out my window. My father turned left and my mother right.

I wondered if Bing had already left for China, angry because I'd said it was impossible. But it wasn't that easy. She'd need a passport and a plane ticket. I didn't believe she'd really gone. She was probably hanging out somewhere on the sidewalk, or she was having a milkshake at the snack bar. When you run away you want to be found. I knew that. I did it once myself. I stood around the corner, shivering in the cold for half an hour. It was the middle of winter and I'd walked out because I'd lost a game of cards. I knew Bing had been cheating.

"What took you so long?" I asked my father when he finally came.

"I thought let's give him a moment to cool off," my father said.

"Weren't you worried?"

"You're still here, aren't you?"

"You didn't know that," I said.

"Of course I knew that," my father said.

That made me so angry that I almost ran away again, but it was too cold. I didn't feel like it anymore.

Something like that was going on with Bing. I'd made her mad and now she was outside somewhere, waiting to be found. But something was bothering me. If I'd made her mad, shouldn't I be the one looking for her?

– – –

I pulled the front door shut behind me and walked toward the park.

"Bing!" I called out as I walked. "Bing!" It sounded silly, like calling a dog.

The park was quiet and dark. I almost didn't dare go on. During the day I wasn't afraid of the bread thief, but I'd rather not meet him at night. Now that I was by myself I kept thinking about that knife. If he had a knife and Bing was in the park...

"Bing!" I shouted as loud as I could. "Bing. Where are you?"

"Fay?" It was a faint call, as if it came from far away. I could barely hear it.

I ran along the path past the aviary. "Bing!"

My feet pounded over the bridge.

Bing was sitting on one of the benches on the other side of the water. The bread thief sat next to her.

"What are you doing here?" Bing asked.

"Everybody's looking for you."

"How did you know I was here?"

"I just came this way," I said. "Like always."

The bread thief took a swig from his beer can. Bing stuck out her hand.

"Don't," I said.

Drinking from the same can as the bread thief was even more gross than kissing.

"Why don't you mind your own business?" the bread thief said.

He passed the can to Bing and Bing emptied it. She held the can upside down. Some beer spilled onto her pants.

"I'm her brother," I said.

The bread thief looked at Bing and then at me and then at Bing again. "Fat chance," he said.

I pulled Bing up.

"Let her go," the bread thief said.

"He really is my brother," Bing said. She dropped the can on the ground.

"Is that so?" the bread thief said. "Are you sure?"

"Don't be difficult," Bing said. "Of course I'm sure."

"I beg your pardon that I didn't believe you right away," the bread thief said.

"We're going home," I said to Bing. "Right now."

Bing was stumbling even more than usual, and it wasn't just because of her high heels.

"Are you drunk?" I asked.

"No," Bing said. She stopped on the bridge. She burped.

"Are you going to barf?" I asked.

"Of course not," Bing said. She had barely said it when she threw up.

"In the water!" I shouted.

It was too late. Bing barfed all over the bridge.

Somebody would have to clean up the mess, but it wasn't going to be me. I felt sick just thinking about it.

Bing looked around for something to hold on to, and I grabbed her by the elbow. I didn't want to touch her hand, because she'd just used it to wipe her mouth.

– – –

My father and mother were waiting at home.

"Bing shouldn't be punished," I said.

"And why not?" my father asked.

"Because it was my fault."

"An," my father said to Bing. "Can you explain this?"

"I don't know," Bing said.

"Have you been drinking?" my mother asked. "I can smell it."

"There were boys," I said, before Bing could mention the bread thief. "They had some beer and because Bing was mad she drank a couple of cans."

"I didn't ask you," my mother said.

"Which boys?" my father asked.

"Just boys," Bing said.

"And girls," I said, because I saw that my father was getting angry about the boys I'd just invented.

"You go to bed," my father said to me.

"But it's my fault that Bing was mad," I said. "That's what matters!"

Slowly my father pushed me out of the room. "We're going to sort out the rest tomorrow. Now go upstairs."

I dragged myself up the stairs, hoping to hear what was going on in the living room. But the door opened again and Bing followed me. She went into the bathroom and I heard her turn on the shower.

— — —

When I was almost asleep she came into my room. Without knocking.

"Fay?" she said.

"Mmm?"

"I don't want you to find your mother."

She sat down at the foot of my bed. I felt the mattress sag a bit.

"But don't mind me. You should find her, even though I don't want you to."

"You're crazy," I mumbled.

— — —

The next morning my mother phoned the Chinese adoption agency and made an appointment with the talk group. Bing wasn't being punished. She was getting help.

I didn't even know there was a Chinese adoption agency with a talk group.

"What do they do there?" I asked Bing.

"They talk, of course."

"Just talk?"

"I think so. You sit in a circle with all these people who are also adopted and also came from China."

If I were Bing I'd go for punishment. A month without horseback riding would be easier.

But Bing thought the talk group was a good idea. "One thing though," she said. "If it's no good, I'll stop right away. And nobody else can join."

"It's a group," I said. "So there are always going to be other people."

"You know what I mean. Dad can't join and Mom can't join and you can't."

"Is there a Bosnian adoption agency too?" I asked my mother.

"No," she said. "There are hardly any adopted children from Bosnia in the Netherlands."

"Lucky me!" I said, feeling greatly relieved.

"Are you happy about that?" my mother asked.

"Nyeah," I said. What would it be like to meet other Bosnian children? Would they all think and feel the same way? If that was true, we'd sit in a circle without saying much. All our brains would be thinking strange thoughts, all at the same time.

– – –

Once a week Bing went to her adoption agency. She refused to talk about it. I could understand that. Talking about a talk group – that was something you'd better not try.

I was waiting for news from Jos. I could call

him, he'd said. But he'd also said he didn't know
how long it would take for mother number zero
to be found. If she was found.

·18·

I was busy. The graduation party was coming up so Hamid and Jesse wanted to practice.

We attached one side of the bed sheet to the wall rack in the gym. We rolled it up and tied it with string. The idea was that Jesse, Hamid and I would walk out together. All three of us in black sweat pants and black T-shirts. I would untie the string and unroll the sheet. Jesse and Hamid would stand in front of it and give a karate demonstration.

"And what should I do?" I asked.

"Roll out the sheet," Hamid said.

"And then?"

"Hold up the sheet," Hamid said.

"And watch the audience and shout once in a while," Jesse said.

"Shout what?" I said. "I have no idea what to shout."

Jesse demonstrated. "Yoi! Kaaaai!" Shout that every time we make a karate hit."

"When you do karate you split something in two," I said. "A pile of bricks or a board."

"We split the sky in two," Hamid said.

"Into a thousand pieces," Jesse said.

I walked to the wall rack and untied the string. Jesse and Hamid swung their arms around.

"Kai," I said.

— — —

We practiced every afternoon. I was still nervous the night of the party, but no one noticed because we were all nervous. I was afraid that I wouldn't be able to loosen the string, and I was afraid that I couldn't shout "Kai!" And what would happen when I rolled out the sheet?

The gym was decorated and the chairs set up in rows. The whole class ate dinner together at school and then we watched the fathers and mothers and other relatives coming in to take their seats.

The evening began with a little speech from Willem. He said what a wonderful class we were. He hadn't had such a wonderful class in years.

Jesse clapped.

"Cut it out," Hamid said.

We were standing with the whole class behind the curtain waiting to perform. No one was supposed to hear us.

There were a lot of karaoke numbers. They came first. I've never understood what's so hot about karaoke. You pretend to sing but everyone can see it's fake. And it makes no sense at all dancing while you're pretending to sing, so it's usually a flop. There was one dance that totally flopped. Nobody minded except the girls who made such a mess of it.

It took a long time before the karaoke numbers were done. I think there were about ten different songs. And then more music. A band with two guitars and a drum set, a band with guitars but no drum set, a saxophone solo and a small choir of three girls who sang all by themselves without anything going wrong. They were fantastic singers. All three just a bit different, but in tune with each other. The audience in the gym clapped as loud as they could. My knees were getting wobbly. After something so beautiful, the karate performance was going to look stupid.

The three of us walked into the gym together— Jesse, Hamid and I. Jesse and Hamid stopped while I went over to the wall rack. I looked at the people sitting on the chairs. My father and mother and Bing were in the second row next to Jesse's father and mother. My father nodded at me.

I fumbled with the string. It wouldn't come undone and I started to pull, but that only made it worse. It was taking way too long. Jesse came over and pushed me away. He pulled the string so hard it broke. I grabbed the sheet and ran backwards to unroll it.

Jesse's mother shot up from her seat. "My bed sheet!" she shouted.

People in the gym stared. There was laughter. "Shit," said Jesse.

Bing wasn't paying attention to Jesse's mother. She stared at the characters – Peace-Loving Ice Baby. She slowly moved her head from side to side as if she was reading it a few times. Then she fixed her eyes on me.

I pointed at the sheet and then I pointed my finger at Bing. "For you," I mouthed.

She just sat there, but I knew her. In just a second she would be furious, and she would jump up and run out of the gym.

For you, I signaled as clearly as possible.

Bing tapped her forehead with her finger. Her lips formed a word that I understood right away — idiot! But she wasn't mad. A broad grin appeared on her face.

Then I did something that nobody expected from me. Something I hadn't expected from myself. I shouted, "Yoi! Kaaaai!"

Suddenly it was silent. We could start. I still had wobbly knees, but it didn't matter because I was standing behind the sheet and hardly anyone was paying attention to me. Everyone was looking at Jesse and Hamid and the movements they made with their arms. I don't think anybody knew what that was supposed to mean. And nobody knew what was painted on the sheet. Nobody except Bing and me. Even my father and mother hadn't figured it out. They watched with open mouths as the sky was chopped into a thousand pieces.

•19•

My father and mother were going to put me to bed together. I thought it was strange, but I'd just finished my last day of middle school and maybe they wanted to make it special. Luckily they didn't come up right away. They stayed downstairs until I'd brushed my teeth.

"It was fun tonight," my mother said when they came up.

"Those girls singing," my father said.

My mother gave him a nudge. "And Fay."

"Of course," my father said. "And Fay."

I got into bed. "Good night," I said.

They were still in my room.

"There's something else," my father said. "Jos called."

"It was a bit awkward," my mother said. "We should have told you right away, but you had your performance coming up and we thought it was better to wait."

"Until it was over," my father said.

I felt a jolt. "What did Jos say?" I asked.

"There's news," my father said. "We'll go see him first thing Monday morning."

"That's two days from now," I said.

"I know, sweetheart," my mother said. "You just have to wait and not get too excited. Jos said there was news, but nothing for sure yet. We shouldn't expect too much."

"Not expect what?"

"That everything has worked out."

"The best thing is to do what Jos says," my father said. "Wait patiently."

"Good night," I said for the second time.

"Shall I stay with you awhile?" my mother asked. "Do you want to talk a bit?"

"No," I said.

It was slightly awkward how my father and mother left the room, as if they didn't really want to go.

"Good night," my father said at the door.

I'd already said good night twice and I thought that was enough. I pulled the covers over my ears.

"If you need anything, just come in," my mother said. "Will you do that?"

"Yes, I will," I said.

I stayed in my bed the whole night. I didn't get out, even though I couldn't sleep. Once in a while I looked at my alarm clock. The time crawled by.

— — —

"You look so tired," my mother said at breakfast. She didn't say much and neither did my father. It seemed like they weren't talking about mother number zero on purpose. Maybe that was a tip from Jos.

Bing was still in bed. I didn't know what to do when she woke up.

"Does Bing know yet?" I asked.

"Yes," my mother said.

"Don't worry too much about Bing," my father said. "You've got enough to think about."

"Can I go outside?" I asked.

My mother suddenly laughed. "Of course you can go outside. You know you never have to ask that!"

"Let's just do everything as usual," my father said.

— — —

I took my sketchbook with me to the ditch next to our house. I tried to draw a swimming duck. I finished in no time. Swimming ducks aren't hard enough. They're like rubber ducks, but alive, and you can't see how they're put together at all because their legs are hidden underwater. I kept walking, and before I knew it I was on my way to the park again.

The sun was shining. There was a woman sitting on my bench. She had pulled up her skirt a bit and stretched her legs out in front of her. The next bench was also taken. A woman with rolled-up pant legs sat there. There were other benches. Enough room. But the women were looking at me and I didn't want to sit down. I went on to the playing field.

From the bridge I could see that Maud was

already there. She had put down a blanket on the grass. She was stretched out on her tummy, reading. I didn't know if I should walk by or not, but she called me.

"Hi!"

I took a large step over Bing's barf stain on the bridge. Somebody had tried to clean it up, but not very well.

Maud moved over a bit and I sat down on a corner of the blanket.

"Where's Jesse?" I asked.

"Jesse is a jerk."

I let her talk.

"He was a jerk all along," Maud said. "Only I didn't know it yet."

She was wearing shorts so I could see her bare legs. They were thin and white. There was a small silver chain around her ankle. The wart under her heel had disappeared.

She turned on her side. "And what about your mother?" she asked.

"I'm going to hear on Monday."

"What are you going to hear?"

"I don't know yet."

"Is it about mother number zero?" Maud asked.

Mother number zero sounded cold. I suddenly realized she needed another name. Maybe I'd shake her hand on Monday and then I'd have to say something. Hello, Mom? No. I didn't want to say Mom. Hello, Ma'am? No. Hello, Mrs. Biological Mother, Mrs. Real Mother, Mrs. Give-Away Mother? It was less scary if I made a game of it. I'm Fay. I'm your give-away kid, your biological Fejzo.

"Yes or no?" Maud asked.

She had the whitest legs I'd ever seen. There was a big blue bruise above one of her knees.

When I didn't say anything, Maud answered herself, "Yes."

I felt like saying, "Get lost." I had to hold back because I was sitting on Maud's blanket, on the spot she had chosen.

"I still have a lot to do," I said.

"Like what?" Maud asked.

"Why don't you get lost," I said quickly.

Maud burst out laughing. "What did you say?"

"Why don't you get lost." I still said it far too fast, in a funny high voice, without meaning to sound that way.

Maud lay flat on her back on the blanket, laughing so hard that I started laughing too. Whatever she thought of me was her business. I didn't care anymore.

— — —

On my way back I walked by the aviary. The women were still there. I acted as if I'd been planning to go to the bandstand all along and followed the path near the duck pond. Halfway there I met the bread thief.

"Hello, brother," he said.

I wanted to say, "Hello, bread thief." I swallowed my words just in time.

"Sir, what's your name?" I asked.

"Sir?" the bread thief said. "Sir? Come on!" He put down his plastic bags. "Anton. That's my name. Antonius, actually."

"Antonius," I said.

"Right," the bread thief said.

— — —

It was quiet at home. My father was doing some errands and my mother was reading the newspaper. I went to the attic. Bing was sitting at the computer.

She moved over a little. "Only five minutes," she warned.

I typed *pelican* on the screen.

"Try this one," Bing said. "Penguin."

"There are no paintings of penguins," I said. "Crow?"

I shook my head.

"Goose," Bing said.

I typed *goose*. The five minutes were long gone.

•20•

Sunday was a long day. I didn't feel like going outside because I didn't want to run into anyone. I didn't feel like talking, not even with my father and mother and not with Bing either. All our conversations were either all about mother number zero or else avoided her on purpose. The conversations that avoided her were the worst, because it was so obvious.

"We should go to Amsterdam sometime," my mother said. "To Waterloo Square. They have boxes full of postcards there."

"Are you still looking for something special?" my father asked me. "Did you know there are endless paintings of sheep? I don't think we've ever found a postcard with a sheep painting."

"No," I said.

"Then we'll go and look for one sometime," my mother said.

— — —

The next morning they didn't talk about paintings of sheep anymore. My father and mother and Bing were waiting at the breakfast table. I sat down and stared at my plate.

"Everything OK?" my father asked.

"Nyeah," I said.

"I don't know the best way to handle this," my mother said. "Dad and I are both coming along, but Bing wants to stay home."

"I don't have to go, do I?" Bing said.

"No, of course not," my father said.

"But you'll be all by yourself," my mother said.

My father picked up his keys. "Let's not make it too complicated," he said. "It's OK."

We got into the car without Bing. My mother drove and I sat in the back with my father. I saw Bing standing upstairs at her bedroom window. When the car drove off she waved.

I leaned a little against my father. He put his arm around my shoulders.

"What am I supposed to do now?" I asked.

"First let's hear what Jos has to say," my father said. "Do you want us to go in with you?"

"Yes," I said. "But Dad, what will happen next? We'll be going on vacation soon."

We were supposed to go to Sweden. My father and mother had rented a cottage near a lake. It was a cottage for four people.

"Does she have to come along?" I asked. "Does mother number zero have to come with us on vacation?"

My father pinched my shoulder. "Of course not."

"But it's so strange to find her and then leave her right away."

My mother was listening. "Sweetheart," she said, "we're not there yet. Not for a long time."

"And you never know what's going to happen," my father said.

Jos had told me about mothers who were found. Sometimes they wanted a lot of contact and sometimes not. There were no hard and fast rules.

— — —

We didn't have to sit in the waiting room very long. Jos came to get us right away. We followed him to his office.

"Well," Jos said when we were all sitting down. "Fejzo, it's an exciting day. Have you been on pins and needles?" There was an envelope on his lap.

"A little bit," I said.

"We've all been nervous," my mother said.

"I understand," Jos said.

"Has she been found?" I asked.

Jos's hands were lying on the envelope. "I'll try to explain it as clearly as possible."

It was a hidden yes, I thought. Or a hidden no. Was she or wasn't she found?

"We know who she is and where she lives."

It was a yes.

"I've talked with her and I've told her about you."

"Yes?" I asked.

"Yes," Jos said. "She was happy."

I looked at the door. Would she come in now? Nothing happened.

"She was glad that you've found such a good home," Jos said. "And she has thought a lot about you."

I glanced at my father and mother. My father smiled and my mother bent over and patted my knee. I swallowed and took a deep breath. It was time to say something to Jos, but I had to swallow again. I had to remember to swallow and breathe and think all at the same time. My brain had to think about what Jos had said, but instead my thoughts were busy with things that are supposed to work by themselves.

"When I told her that you were looking for her, it became difficult," Jos said. "You should know she has gone through a lot. She didn't want to talk too much about it, but it's clear that the situation in Bosnia…" He glanced at my father and mother and then at me again. "Sometimes it takes a long time to deal with something."

My throat hurt from swallowing. Jos's voice came from far away.

"But what happened?" I asked.

"I don't know if we should talk about that right now," my mother said.

"We simply can't talk about it," Jos said to me. "She told me almost nothing. But we know that horrible things happened in Bosnia. Your biological mother was confused, and she thought she wouldn't be able to take proper care of you. When you were born, she was alone and she didn't have a place to stay. Her head was full of war, that's how she expressed it. She didn't want you to suffer because of it."

"Does she live in the Netherlands?" my mother asked. "Does she have a place to live now?"

"Yes," Jos said. "As far as her living situation is concerned, everything is fine."

"That's good to know," my mother said.

"That's all I can tell you," Jos said. "Her address needs to stay secret."

I knew that Jos wasn't supposed to give out mother number zero's address. He'd already explained that to me. He'd told me what usually happened when he was looking for a mother. First of all he had to find out what she herself wanted, and he wasn't allowed to tell everything about her. But it was still strange. Jos knew mother number zero's address and I didn't. He already knew what mother number zero looked like.

"So then I can't go and see her," I said.

"Maybe this is a bit hard for you to hear," Jos said. "But she doesn't want to meet you. Not yet. It's too difficult. Later, she said, when she's feeling better and you're a little older."

"Why?" I asked.

"Because she needs time," Jos said. "Because she has to think more and because you're part of the past, she said. And the past is still too close. Do you understand that?"

"A little," I said.

"We'll talk more about it later," Jos said. "I'm sorry. Maybe this isn't the answer you were hoping for."

"No," I said. But actually I wasn't quite sure what I'd hoped for.

"It's an unusual situation," Jos said. "She's not saying yes or no. She's saying yes, but not yet. Or no, but maybe later." He took the envelope from his lap. "She gave me this. It's for you."

I took the envelope and held it in my hands.

"It's a photo," Jos said. "You can take it home with you or you can look at it right now. Whatever you want. We can leave you alone for a moment if you like."

"Or we can stay with you," my mother said.

"Can I leave for a moment?" I asked.

"Are you sure?" Jos asked. "Is that OK?"

My mother pushed her chair back. "Why don't you go?"

I walked past the waiting room and turned a corner. There was a coffee machine and next to it a wooden bench. I sat down and tore open the envelope. I carefully lifted out the photo.

•21•

She looked like me.

No, it was the other way around, of course. I looked like her.

She had honey eyes. Brown, but not brown enough. As if they ran out of eye color when she was made. She had hair down to her shoulders, a bit darker than mine. A half-smiling mouth, as if she wasn't quite sure she wanted to smile.

Her head didn't look like it was full of war. But Jos was probably right. She had to think it over, he'd said. She needed time. Maybe her head wasn't just full of war. Maybe she had my kind of brain too. Or I had hers. A brain with thoughts that went all over the place and couldn't give quick answers. A brain that took a bit longer to work.

I stuck my hand in the envelope. I hoped there would be a letter inside, but it was empty. I turned the photo over. On the back something was written in pencil – *For Fejzo from A.*

That was all. No name, only A.

I turned the photo over again and looked at mother number zero's face. For the very first time I looked like someone. When I looked at the photo I saw a little bit of myself at the same time.

I felt a lump in my throat. And my eyes stung. I thought about all the terrible things I had imagined – mother number zero with a knife in the park, mother number zero with bobbing breasts in the train, and mother number zero who never washed herself because she painted all day long.

I knew what I should call her now– mother A. Mother A was better than mother number zero.

•22•

I went home with my father and mother. This time my father drove and I sat in the back with my mother.

My mother looked at the photo.

"Ah," she said. "You look so much like her."

"Strange, isn't it?" I said.

My mother put the photo back in the envelope. "Was it a big shock?"

I shrugged my shoulders.

"And now she doesn't want to meet you. You knew that something like this could happen, but still…"

I looked out the window.

"Everything OK back there?" my father asked.

"Oh yes," I said.

"It's all right to feel sad," my mother said.

"I'm not sad," I said.

She gave me a kiss.

— — —

At home I took the photo up to my room. I didn't know what to do with it. A photo should be put or hung somewhere so that you can look at it. Every time I saw mother A's face my heart started to beat a little faster. With shock and amazement and uneasiness. I didn't want that feeling all the time. The face of mother A was a face to look at once in a while. And imagine having that picture hanging in my room. Then everyone could see it. If someone came over I'd have to explain who mother A was. And when my mother came up to vacuum she'd see another mother.

My book of animals was lying on my desk. I opened it. The last pages were still empty. I got my glue and spread it along the top edge of the photo. Only the very top, because I didn't want to spoil mother A's writing. I glued the picture on the first empty page. I didn't write anything down. That wasn't necessary.

Now the book of animals wasn't a book of animals anymore. I leafed through it — *The Hare* by Dürer, *The Goldfinch* by Fabritius, *The Pissing Cow* by Nicolaes Berchem and all the other postcards I had pasted in. Near the end were the dead fish and *Red Squirrel* by Hans Hoffmann. And then suddenly the head of mother A. Something wasn't right. But I didn't mind.

— — —

Halfway through the afternoon Bing came to my room.

"Can I come in?" she asked.

"You already have," I said.

She sat down on my bed. "I think it's so stupid," she said.

"It's all right."

"Not."

"How do you know?"

Bing sighed, "Aren't you angry?"

"At who?"

"At your mother," Bing said. She leaned back with her head against the wall.

I wasn't angry.

"What are you going to do?"

"Nothing," I said.

It was true. I wasn't going to do anything. I didn't have to do anything.

Nothing! Mother A didn't want to meet me. She had told Jos it was still too difficult. It was something I couldn't explain to Bing. Mother A was right. It was still too difficult. And because it was still too difficult, everything would get a lot easier now. I didn't have to think about what to say to mother A. I didn't have to think about what I should do. No more thinking about all the things that might or might not happen. There was so much I could let go of now.

"Why are you grinning?" Bing said.

"Just because," I said.

Mother A would know what should come next. Later. Later was still far away.